Diamond Dust

How A Nice Mormon Boy Became A Brilliant Counterfeiter

Russ Swain

— WITH —

Michael McKinley

First printing, July 2024
Library of Congress Control Number: 2023950669
ISBN 978-1-953136-72-5 Hardback
ISBN 978-1-953136-73-2 Paperback
ISBN 978-1-953136-82-4 Audiobook

Cover Design by Kurt Lovelace
Cover Artwork by Pierian Springs Press
Cover type *Bauhaus Dessau* **Alfarn** by Céline Hurka,
Elia Preuss, Flavia Zimbardi,
Hidetaka Yamasaki, and Luca Pellegrini.
Body & Chapter Titles set in **No 9T**
Headers in **Jenson** by Robert Slimbach
Flourishes set in Emigre Foundry **Dalliance,** by Frank Heine &
Emigre Foundry **ZeitGuys,** by Bob Aufuldish, Eric Donelan.
Typefaces licensed Adobe, Linotype, & URW GmbH.

PSPress.Pub
Pierian Springs Press, Inc
30 N Gould St, Ste 30
Sheridan, Wyoming 82801

"Everything you can imagine is real."

Pablo Picasso

Contents

Diamond Dust

The Moment When Everything Changed

I never set my sights on becoming a criminal, but you could say my life of crime all began with a postage stamp.

That would be true, and also, not completely accurate. It all depends on how you see the world.

How we see the world, and each other, is at the heart of my story, but not in some uplifting spiritual way, though I am not opposed to that route either, and I have often traveled along it.

No, the way I think about seeing is simple: we all see what we want to see. As an artist, I have the added advantage of making you see the world the way that I have presented it. You look at what I show you, a reality that I have sprinkled with diamond dust, of which you shall soon learn the wonders. I humbly ask you to trust that the diamond dust will please you, and that so will my story of what it all means.

I am an artist, though I am also a counterfeiter, which means I am also a con artist. What does that mean? The term is a shortening of "confidence artist" which describes someone who makes you believe that what they are telling you, or selling you, is real.

Of course, if it exists in words or deeds, it is real. The confidence part of the artist is making you believe that their lies or their forgeries are more than just real but that they are "true."

Which, of course, raises all kinds of questions about the nature of truth. If I tell you that a painting that I have done is by Pablo Picasso, and to your eye, that looks true, then there is only a legal issue with it if I also attempt to sell you that painting as a genuine Picasso. But we can admire it together as the work of the Spanish genius, and is there harm in that?

Same with counterfeit money. If you believe that the $20 bill which I hand you is true, and you give me goods in exchange for it, and then use that $20 bill yourself, have I committed a crime? Or have I simply injected my reality into another one? We shall see, but when I use the term con artist, I use it with an emphasis on the confidence that I have in my own artistry to make you see the truth that I want you to see. And which, I hope, will inspire you.

So, that postage stamp was not my first attempt to make the world see what I wanted it to see, and I will get into my childhood adventures in manufacturing reality as we go, but it was my first adult attempt to do so. And it was successful in itself, and well beyond, and it was what led me to create more realities, some of them better than others.

Here's what happened. When I graduated from art school in the early 1970s, I realized that there must be thirty of us graduating art students who were competing for maybe the one art job in Ogden, Utah, with this little company called Pierson and Kearney Advertising. And so that's when I thought I needed something to make my resumé stand out.

I had grown up in Ogden, a very classy little town nestled right between the Great Salt Lake and the Wasatch Mountain. It was small, with a population of around 150,000 in the early 1970s, and it was a very upbeat place with a main street, called Washington Boulevard. My mother would get dressed up in her fancy coat and go down to Washington Boulevard to go shopping. You will meet her in a little bit.

As soon as you start climbing up closer to the mountain in Ogden, that's where you find the snobby people. The higher you could get a house up the mountain, the more prestige you had, but Ogden was a pretty dynamic town from the lowest point at which you stood, and that's where I stood when I decided to do something highly original and truly illegal to apply for that art house job.

We could call this my Rubicon moment. You know, that moment when Julius Caesar crossed the Rubicon river with his army in the 1st century BCE. A general taking his army, intact, into another Roman territory was an act punishable by death. Caesar did it, and his crossing became the catalyst for a civil war, and it began his rule as a dictator, or Caesar. And eventually, the Rubicon crossing led to his violent death.

In other words, once he had crossed it, there was no going back.

I did not cross any Utah rivers nor start any civil wars and make myself Caesar. What I did was to do something very simple and small, and from that one action, you could say my life as a counterfeiter truly began.

As luck would have it, this ad agency was looking for an art director. They had requested the applicants to send resumes, but not to send any portfolio work. If you couldn't send any work in, then how could I show them my art? I had to find a way to show my work, without showing my work in order to stand out in a sea of competing resumes.

And just like that, I figured out a way to do that very thing. So, I sent them my resume with a cover letter attached. That letter said to its dear reader this: "The fact that you're reading my resume right now is a testament of my capabilities to creatively think outside of the box because I hand-painted the postage stamp that is on the envelope in which it arrived." In other words, if they were reading the letter, then my hand-painted stamp had fooled the U.S. Postal Service and made it through their mighty system.

It was the U.S. Postal Service which had inspired me in the

first place. At the time, they had decided to change up their stamps from commemorating dead presidents and brought out a line of really cool looking postage stamps featuring exotic butterflies. The butterfly stamps were enthralling. I thought they were so beautiful with intricate patterns marked on their luminous wings, that I almost wanted to copy one.

As I was putting together my resumé this wild idea just popped into my head. Why don't I copy one of those gorgeous butterfly stamps on the envelope which will contain my resumé? It would be an eye-catching kind of thing to do, especially if the stamp made it through to the recipient.

The stamp was worth maybe thirteen cents, and I spent much more than that in my time and supplies to make my own stamp. I used these tiny sable brushes to capture the detail of the butterfly that I painted directly onto the envelope which would hold my resume.

But there was another issue. The stamp that I had painted on the envelope was not three dimensional, as it would have been had I just pasted an ordinary postage stamp onto the envelope. I had to figure out a way to make my counterfeit stamp look three dimensional, and so, to look real.

Using the finest brush I had, I painted a touch of light along the upper edge of the stamp and a tiny hint of a shadow at the bottom. It looked as if you rubbed your hand along it, you would feel a ridge, because you could see the ridge with the light at the top and the shadow at the bottom and so you would believe that the stamp was three dimensional, and so, a real stamp.

I knew that if my application made it through the postal service to Pierson and Kearney Advertising and whomever opened my envelope would rub their fingers over my stamp, they would see that it was flat, and not dimensional. They would see that I had painted it to look like it had been pasted on top. They would see my art. And I was confident it could pass the inspection of the keen-eyed postal people and make it all the way to the desk of the person doing the hiring.

The whole project was just a game to me more than being any

criminal attempt to avoid paying for a stamp. But to my pleasure, and a touch of surprise, my resume made it through the mail and into the hands of the ad agency director, who called me. He said that what I had done was pretty creative. Not only that, but he also wanted me on their team. And so, I got the job, in large part because of a counterfeit postage stamp.

I worked at the agency for a couple of years. They were the "go to" people for Ogden's banks and businesses, building ad campaigns for them and so on, but I was basically working as a layout artist: designing brochures, doing logo design, and building catalogs.

It was like being the architect of the printed page, back before the personal computer made everyone an architect. Eventually, I felt confident enough to leave the agency, and to hang out my own shingle in a little strip mall here in a suburb of Ogden called Riverdale. We added typesetting equipment to design posters and flyers and brochures, and people were coming to us to get typesetting done because, as I said, this was before Steve Jobs had perfected that computer thing he was working on in his garage.

Then I thought, people have got to get this stuff that I am designing printed. Why don't we put it in a print shop as well? And so, we had a little printing press installed, and things were moving along quite nicely. I called my business Para Graphics.

In fact, starting that business is how I met my wife, who is no longer my wife, due to the story I am telling you here. But I did not know that then. The printer whom I will call John, I met while doing freelance graphic design projects that I needed to be printed. If I designed a brochure or a letterhead, I would take them to his little print shop and let him work his magic.

I walked into John's shop one day to see that he had this young lady working for him. She had come over from Hawaii for a visit, and now needed a job, so she could get the money to fly back home. She was the prettiest young lady I had ever laid my eyes on since I was twelve years old and blowing up wasps. I was still the fair-haired Mormon boy at the time, which is not to say I was some kind of blond man-god, but I was not in want of women to date, either. Even so, I kept coming back to John's shop for any reason I could dream up. I designed letterheads for non-existent clients just so I could see this woman who was a vision of celestial wonder happily came from a Mormon military family and had spent time in places around the world. Not only was she gorgeous, but she was also worldly.

One of my friends said, "If you're so taken with her, why don't you ask her out?" I thought she was on a much higher plane of existence than me (I would turn out to be right) but I got bold, and I asked her out. She said yes. Then I asked her if she wanted to quit working for John and come to work with me. She said yes.

Indeed, it was art that sealed the deal for me with her. I just really admired an artist named David Lance Goines. When I started dating the woman who would become my wife, I also was dating another girl. This other girl and I drove up to Logan, which is 40 miles from Ogden, to see a movie. As we were walking out of the movie theater, I saw this poster in this little shop. It stopped me in my tracks. I said to her, "Oh my God, look at that beautiful poster!" It was by David Lance Goines, and the subject matter was an antique car with an elegant halo around it.

I thought it was the most brilliant, spectacular piece of graphic design, and I was just moved by it. And this girl looked blankly at me and said, "Well, what about it?"

I was thinking, ahh, she doesn't get it. So, the very next day, I invited the woman who would become my wife to drive with me to Logan. We're going to go to this little restaurant, and our walk to it would take us past that shop with the Goines poster in it. I wanted to see what her reaction was, but I didn't give her any advance intelligence on the mission.

So, we were walking along the street, and we passed the shop, and she grabbed my arm, and said "You've got to stop! Look at this poster!" It was the poster I loved. I looked at it, and I was smiling like a man who had found true love. I thought that's it. Forget the other girl. This is the woman for me. We bought the poster. Indeed, that poster now hangs in the home of one of our daughters.

I was so impressed that I wanted to go to meet this Goines guy, and he too, contributes to my story. He had a little atelier in Los Angeles, called St. Hieronymus press, and I had reason to go to California. So, I called him and asked if I could drop in to see his shop. And he said, "Come on by!" So, I did. He was about four years older than me, but he looked like he had stepped out of Paris in the 1920s. He had a shaved head and this incredibly lush walrus mustache and the look of a kindly wizard in his eyes. He also had this old-style printing press, which did not do half tones or pixelated things. Everything he did was in a single, solid color.

He explained his art to me. "This line here," he said, "is kind of a wiggly, because I don't use really straight lines. Think of it this way: if you had a piece of string, a wiggly string has more string in it. I figure a wiggly line has more density."

I was so inspired by him that I asked what advice he might give to a young fledgling artist who was just starting out as a graphic designer. He said, "You don't even have to write this down, put your pen away. You'll remember this forever. My advice to you is to steal with both hands."

And I said, "I'm not sure if I understand."

He replied "Never sacrifice quality for the sake of originality. Look for references. You're going off about this great poster that I did. But I stole it from a European guy named Albert Bandura. And I was even more impressed when I found out that he stole the composition from this other guy, you know, 50 years earlier. That's what artists do; they steal with both hands. You know, Picasso himself said, 'good artists borrow, great artists steal.' " Then he smiled and stroked that walrus mustache. "You know, no other industry is so hung up on originality," he said, "Think about it. Would you want an original dentist?"

Those words were certainly with me as I set out to make my name in the world of graphic design, and soon I would understand just how deeply embedded they were. I was now married and had a young family, but in the interest of protecting the innocent, I am not going to dwell on my lovely wife or my two gorgeous daughters, born just a year apart. I am leaving them as much out of my story as I can because they didn't know what I was shortly about to get up to. If their presence or deeds are germane to what I am revealing, they shall be revealed a little bit, as they are now, since I had to support them with my work.

My plan with Para Graphics was to set the world on fire not as an arsonist, but as an artist. When I landed the gig to make the brochures for a college which had branches in Utah and across the country that helped adults get their college degrees, I pretty much figured that if I got this one right, the job would put me on the graphic design map, and I would be flooded with offers. And I would achieve success and kindle the flames of interest far and wide in me and my work.

To do the job the way I imagined doing it, I needed to buy some better equipment for my shop from John, the printer who had introduced me to my wife. The brochure for these colleges that I saw dancing in my mind's eye was something like you'd get for an ocean cruise line, with full color printing and clean strong lines. We had to farm out some of the color printing, along with other tech things, so there were other contractors that we had to pay. As a result, I needed to borrow $10,000 to make the project the success that I knew it could be.

Now $10,000 in 1983 is worth $30,410 in 2023 currency. Most people don't have that kind of money lying around, and I was like most people. I had to get it from somewhere, and the bank was not an option because I didn't have enough equity in anything to act as collateral for them to be interested in helping me out.

So, I turned to a loan shark. "Shark" was a term from the late 16th century that meant a "dishonest person who preys on others," and by the turn of the 20th century it had evolved, or devolved, to describe someone who loaned people money and charged them a high rate of interest for the privilege of borrowing it. I met my loan shark through my friend Richie, from high school, who owned and operated a small T-shirt printing business. Tommy the Shark was a wholesaler who sold blank t-shirts to many of the Utah T-shirt vendors, and he sold them to

Richie.

Rather than extend credit to a dry goods company, for a modest percentage fee, Tommy would loan shark the money upfront to the client at the usurious interest rate of 10% per month. Then you could use that money to pay cash to his company for the shirts, print them, and then pay the money back with the added interest that you collected from your client when they bought your T-shirts. The clients paid back your loan.

I went to Tommy and told him that I had this big brochure deal which would be very good for my business. I needed to borrow $10,000 for a month on the certainty that the college would love my brochure and promptly pay me and all would be well. Tommy said great, but that I needed to understand the reality of his loan: he charged interest at 10% per month. "If you go past thirty days, you'll owe me another thousand on top of the ten," he said.

I was sweating a little bit, because that was some serious money to a young guy like me, then in my mid-thirties, with, as I mentioned, a wife and two young children to support. I wasn't sweating because Tommy was physically intimidating. He was just shy of forty years old, and about five-foot-nine, with a medium build, thinning brown hair combed back on his head, and a thick, Teddy Roosevelt kind of mustache on his broad, strong face. He wasn't Hulk Hogan, so I didn't feel he would beat me to smithereens if I failed to pay.

I was sweating because he instilled fear in me with this look in his eye, like that of a hunter, who was always on guard against a threat or danger as he stalked his prey. I tried not to show that I was intimidated, but he knew that I was.

He only had one friend that I knew of. And he was a guy named Rhino (due to a shortening of his last name, and not his size), who I had heard was a total sociopath.

He and Tommy had been the closest of friends after high school and had shared an apartment together. But Rhino, showing his socio colors, would 'bird-dog' the girls that Tommy dated which put them on a competitive course, and which only amped up their macho challenges to each other.

Tommy had backed Rhino on some real estate projects, and they had both made money. They were like a cobra and a mongoose constantly circling each other, waiting for the other one to strike. It gave them each some kind of thrill.

Tommy the Shark was married, with children, so he had let someone else get close to him, at least twice. He was totally committed to his wife, Launi, which is why it was so curious that the only place he insisted that we meet, to arrange and conduct business, was at Happy Trails, a high end "gentlemen's club" in downtown Salt Lake City, where he lived. Tommy did his business out of a stripper bar.

The club was no Gothic palace that you might see in some other sin city, like Vegas or Manhattan. No, it was a windowless one storey strip joint appropriately in a strip mall in the northern part of the city not too far from the airport, in case you wanted to see some almost naked women before you flew off to wherever.

The bar was where Tommy could read his opponents because they were distracted by the strippers. He would study whoever he was doing business with, to look for clues as to their weaknesses, while they gaped at the antics on stage. This world was not part of my Mormon travels as I was a little bit more than embarrassed at being in a stripper bar because I wasn't used to it. And I wasn't supposed to be here.

I was out of my element, and I was being sized up by Tommy as I tried not to ogle the writhings of ample-breasted strippers who might have been nice Mormon girls gone wrong. But then, I was there, too, so we were in this together. I could not look away from these voluptuous young women getting almost naked before me, as the laws at the time compelled them to keep their G-strings on.

Which is exactly what Tommy wanted. I felt like I was being played, and of course, I was. Tommy never looked at the strippers, ever, and I was in that club with him a few times. It was his way of showing that these naked women had no power over him, so he was in control. He was in a stripper bar, but he didn't care about watching the show.

I just wanted to get out of there fast. Good Mormons don't drink alcohol, so I was sipping a cola at $5 a glass, while Tommy, who was also a Mormon by birth, was drinking beer. He had no time for religion or politics or anything that could get in the way of him running the show, so he was not thinking at all about breaking any tenets of the faith into which he was born because he had no connection to it.

I badly wanted to wrap things up and Tommy was enjoying my discomfort. "Sit back and relax, Swain," he said, as he always called me by my last name. "I'm gonna finish my beer." Then he drank that beer very slowly. He was not out to get drunk. He was making a point.

In the end, I got my $10,000 from Tommy the Shark, and I knew that I was going to make the college brochure that would change my life, and that of my young family—and that I would pay Tommy back before his punishing interest kicked in. I was, in fact, going to be rich.

The company that ran the colleges for whom I was designing the brochure was a big deal. When their New York office called me, they said, "We want you to design this splashy brochure that we're going to use nationwide." I knew that this job would take me out of Utah into the great market of the entire country. I was going to go national.

I had sent the school a comprehensive mock-up of the brochure, using sketched characters, showing the positioning of the models. They approved the layout, and the brochure went into full production.

It was the early 1980s, so I thought 'What would a national company that ran colleges want to show to prospective students?' I kept coming back to the same answer, and it was perfect: everyone was welcome in their academic world.

In my brochure, I featured two students. One was an athletic Asian guy, and the other was an attractive African American woman. I wanted anyone who saw the brochure to see America, and to feel that these colleges were the right place for them.

The brochure I made for the company made me proud, and I was certain the company would love how I had created a diverse image of them at a time when diversity was nowhere near the social reality that it is today. So, I was shocked when the president of the company called me from New York and shouted a question at me. "Are you playing some kind of a joke on us?"

No, I was not, I told him. He was furious, and he told me that my contract with his company was dead and buried, because I had dared to put—and here he used two very offensive racial epithets which I will not repeat—in his brochure. The school had gone to great lengths to appeal to the white collar, white upper class and my brochure had laid down the welcome mat for those less desirable groups. He only wanted white people, and I was too stupid to understand that, so I was fired.

I was shocked. How could he even think like that and run a national college company? That thought was soon crowded out by another more alarming thought: how am I ever going to pay Tommy the Shark the $10,000 that I owed him? Because very soon, when the interest kicked in, it was going to be $11,000. And then it would be piling up fast.

I was alone in my shop, and it was a Friday evening. I had a few weeks until Tommy the Shark came looking for his money. My wife and children were away for the week, as it was summer. I had no one other than myself to be with, and so, that's where I went.

My mind traveled back to the other times when I had to think out of the box creatively, and I thought about the postage stamp I had counterfeited to get me the job with the ad agency. What else could I copy to get myself out of this money jam I was in?

I could copy a famous painting, and sell it on the art market, but that would take too much time, and maybe I wouldn't even find a buyer. I mean, I knew how to fake a Picasso, and I could find a way to sell it, and indeed one day I would do that very thing. But right here and now, I did not have a long list of counterfeit Picasso buyers in my Rolodex.

I could do trompe l'oeil work for rich people up in Park City, and design eye-tricking murals for them. The thing is, I did not yet know any such people, though I would do one day, and I would get paid for my art tricks.

No, I had to come up with something fast and simple. So, I took out my wallet and looked at a $20 bill.

It was as if a bright light went off in my head. I thought, there's a company called Cranes that manufactures the paper used to print U.S. currency. It's 100% cotton with a silk content gives the paper more durability, and even better, I happened to have a couple of reams of that paper in my shop because I was using it to design an attorney's letterhead.

Then I thought, what about the color of the paper? My mind was racing as I followed the idea burbling up in my head. And I was staring at the answers that would fuel the journey. I had a printing press, so I knew that I could just print the background color to match the $20. I've got a pretty good color perception, and I could make some ink, and I could just paint a full bleed on this 100% cotton rag paper made by Cranes, the Treasury people. So, I had figured out the paper, and the color. But as I stared at the $20 bill, I thought the problem was the little red and blue fibers going through the background of the bill. And I thought, 'how can I fake those?'

And then, in a flash, the answer popped out in my head. A smile spread across my face. I knew how I could counterfeit a $20 bill. Would it work? There was only one way to find out. So, I went outside and slapped a sign on my door that I was away on vacation.

Then I went back inside my shop, and I took the first steps to raise my career as a counterfeiter to the next level. I was going to fake $20 bills. At first, it was just to pay Tommy the Shark back. But as I would soon discover, once you have tasted success—and I would feast on it—then it is very hard to leave the table. Unless someone makes you. And that happened too, as you shall soon find out.

2

How I Got
To the Moment
When Everything Changed

I came into this world in a very artistic manner, especially if the artist you're thinking of is Andy Warhol. I was born in a can of Pork & Beans.

My parents, Lester and Melba, started out together in a very small, northern Utah town called Roosevelt. Dad used to say that the population of Roosevelt never changed because every time a young woman got pregnant, some guy would leave town.

But Dad, bless him, went against the demographic practice, and stuck around when my mother was pregnant with me. There wasn't a hospital in Roosevelt that was suitable for birthing babies back in 1949, so on the night of November 3, when I started to kick my little bones into the world, my parents had to drive their old Hudson to the nearest hospital, which meant a drive to Salt Lake City.

Dad had made a makeshift bed on the back seat for my Mom, who was propped-up on pillows to make her four-hour trip to the hospital in comfort. Also in that back seat was an empty, half-gallon sized Pork & Beans can, to be used when Dad needed to add water to the radiator.

As Dad neared the hospital, a different kind of fluid landed in that Pork & Bean can as Mom's water broke, and so she held that can under her to catch the contents. Dad pulled up to the entrance of the hospital, stopped the car and ran inside, yelling to the staff, "My wife's giving birth in the backseat of the Hudson out here!"

When he got back to Mom, my little head had emerged and I was face-down in the middle of that can, becoming one of the first, if not exactly "Campbell's Soup Kids", then the prototype. Russ Swain, the Pork & Beans Baby.

My mother, Melba, was an artist, and my father, Lester, was a house painter. My mother had left small town Utah for Los Angeles as a young woman to make her way in the art world. At the time, in the mid-1930s, Los Angeles was the fifth largest city in the U.S., with a population of one and a quarter million people. If you wanted to test your talents and stay fairly close to home in Utah, Los Angeles was the place to be.

My mother was very attractive, with fine features and silky brown hair, and she drew lots of attention from men. So, when this dapper guy, in his mid-thirties, with a thick black mustache and wearing an ascot, came up to her at a party in Los Angeles, she was prepared for another predictable seduction attempt from some ruthless LA playboy. He introduced himself and said "My name is Walt Disney. I know that name doesn't mean anything to you. But I bet you've heard of my mouse."

My mother was surprised at his pick-up technique, as this was the first time anyone had invoked a mouse, so she backed away from him. He said, "No, no, no, no, I've got a mouse in my animation studio! But animation is a cheap parlor trick! The difference with me is that my mouse can talk!"

Disney had just sold Mickey Mouse to the movies, and he had moved on to what he called his "dream project". He said it would be the first full length animated feature film, and he talked Melba Gardner into going to work for him on this film as a production artist. So, she said yes, and that is how she wound up doing artwork on the Disney film *Snow White and the Seven Dwarfs*.

She took me to the movie every time it came into town, and when her work appeared on screen she would proclaim, with pride, "This is the scene that I did!" It was the scene where Snow White has a broom in hand and she's sweeping the hearth of the fireplace with the help of bunnies and a bird. It is an iconic scene, and today, you can buy a kid size version for your tot to play in for $350! It was, and is, to me, the finest scene in the film.

She also told me stories about Walt Disney and pork and beans, so we have a connection there as well. He would eat them out of a can with a spoon, as he pleaded with his brother Roy to make payroll every weekend. He would pep talk about a character idea he had—to his brother, and to himself—and say "Don't give up on this one, it's going to work! I swear it's going to work!"

My mother only stayed with Disney for about six months. She dated some wealthy California guys, who would have been happy to keep her in California, but in the end, she wanted to come back to Utah. She wanted to marry someone of her Mormon faith and settle down to a quiet life as an art teacher in the public school system.

She was forty-six years old when I was born, so you could say I was a bit of a miracle child. She had already given birth to my brother Larry four years earlier when my dad was away doing military service. My dad wasn't there when my older brother was born. But he was there when I was born in that Pork & Beans can.

My brother felt, as a 4-year-old kid, that I was this interloper who kind of pushed him out of the crib. My father was never that close with my brother because he was away with the army and missed his formative first years growing up and so, I became the favorite kid and that made my brother want to strangle me in my crib. He was no longer the king of the hill, and although I always liked him, we never learned how to become close. There was always some distance between us, so we kept mostly to ourselves.

So, given that my brother Larry more or less absented himself from my childhood, I became my mother's golden boy. And having an older mother was great. Her wisdom was deep and her talents as a person and as an artist had already fully developed. I was lucky.

She was my art teacher as well, and while my father would give me useful aphorisms such as "It's easier to get into a situation than out of one," my mother would teach me the means which I could use to create my own situation through art.

Of course, kids are always creating their own realities, as their brains are still under construction, and in the summer when I was entering the fifth grade, I displayed a bravery, or maybe a bravado, that showed how my take on reality was already following its own path which, in this instance, was literally explosive.

That fifth grade summer, I had learned from some older kids that you can make a small rocket, fueled by a propellant which you made by melting brown sugar in a saucepan on the stove. When that sugar is molten, you pour in a bunch of saltpeter, then stir it around and let it cool. Now you've got some good rocket fuel.

We assembled a rocket out of empty cans of concentrated fruit juice. The bottom can contained the propellant, and I fashioned a nose cone and fins from light cardboard, then made a stand from a metal rod, and when all that was done, put a match to the fuse and that sucker took-off like, well, a rocket.

Of course, we were inspired to do more. We learned that

we could create small bombs by crushing Kellogg's Frosted Flakes and combining them with bat guano, which is the excrement produced by bats and used as fertilizer. By coincidence, my dad knew of a cave in Northeastern Utah, which was home to thousands of bats. He would drive there and fill five-gallon paint buckets with bat guano to use as fertilizer in his garden, due to its high content of nitrogen, phosphate, and potassium, all needed in abundance for healthy plant growth.

My best friend Denny, who was in the same grade as me and lived on the next block over, would dip into my father's bat guano supply with me as we continued our education in backyard chemistry, because bat guano is also used in gunpowder. Once we had learned how to make small bombs, then we wanted to blow stuff up. We also realized that you have to hate whatever you blow up—otherwise, what's the point?

In the vacant lots and alleyways of Ogden there existed mounds of red fire-ants. If you've ever been bitten by a fire ant, it hurts like hell. I had been bitten a few times, and I hated fire ants. So, we'd find an anthill, and bury our little bombs beside it, then light the fuse and run because the explosion blew sand, pebbles, and fire ants, all over the place.

That same summer, one of my mom's school-teacher friends in the neighborhood, stopped by our house to visit. In the course of the conversation, she mentioned that she had been stung by a wasp from a large nest that hung from the eaves of her garage. She was afraid of wasps and wasn't sure how to get rid of the nest.

She also had a gorgeous twelve-year-old daughter—the same age as me. She was the most exotic creature that I had ever seen, with jet black hair and the bluest of eyes and she was, from a distance, the goddess who I worshiped. Let's call her Clio. I knew how I could get Clio to notice me in a way that would change my life forever.

I assured my mother's teacher pal with her beautiful Clio that I had a bug bomb that would do the trick in eradicating those evil wasps and make their world safe. She gave me an enthusiastic yes, please! So, I mixed everything from my shelf of chemicals into my concoction, then packed it in a small can of cardboard, and wrapped tape around it to make it look like a more professional kind of bomb. With Clio and her mother watching from a distance, I made my heroic climb up the step ladder and taped the bomb near the wasp nest. I lit the fuse, then jumped off the ladder and ran toward Clio.

A bright flash of white light, accompanied by a deafening pop, sent wood splinters in every direction as the eaves exploded. Words, both profane and holy, flew from the teacher's mouth! In fact, up to that point, I had never considered that our Lord and Savior might even have a middle name. From my own mouth, came profanity too, a short word for excrement.

Smoke billowed, the fire department came, and Clio looked at me like I was from one of those schools where they sent kids who weren't quite right in the head. My father ended up re-constructing the eaves of her garage. My mother made a cake and took it over to her house and it ended well, if you can call Clio never speaking to me again a happy ending. My father's take on it all has stayed with me: "He's the only kid I know who could screw up a junk yard," he said, shaking his head at this failure which he had produced.

Maybe that's why my father was always trying to get me involved in his house painting, with that old chestnut that "it might be something you can fall back on one day." I didn't want to be a house painter because I wasn't planning on falling. I had shifted my vision from bomb making to art, which was safer. And I was going to be an artist someday, while not yet realizing there's a reason that the word "starving" generally precedes the word "artist".

My brother Larry's art was photography, so both my

brother and I had that artistic vision. The painter and the photographer both have to choose a subject, to choose a reality that they are going to try to reveal. And in that choice, we can change how the viewer sees that reality through our own interpretation of it.

Think of looking at a full moon in the clear night sky. You can hold up a quarter at arm's length, and block out that moon, even though a quarter is minuscule when compared to the moon's diameter of more than two thousand miles. But from where we stand, with that quarter in hand, we can change our perspective and make that big moon very small. And in that choice, we can change how we see reality. Do we really see what we think we're seeing?

That reality change is something that has always fueled my artistic imagination. The artist's choice to paint this, and not that, is the first step in creating a reality. And once the artist has made that choice, the control is theirs. You have to look where I am looking. And see what I have allowed you to see.

Looking back now, I see our household was what you might call a "situation" that I was stuck in. My mother married my father thinking he was a good Mormon guy. But he was also an alcoholic. And he was a mean drunk when he got drunk—not beating us to a pulp or anything like that, but verbally mean, making us feel small. My mother would try to intervene, even by dumping his bottles of booze down the sink, but it didn't stop him. So, there was always this tension in our household.

My mother was pushing me to be religious, because it was important to her, and so I was. This meant adhering to the tenets of the faith like not smoking, drinking alcohol or having unmarried sexual relations. And going to church three times on Sundays. My mother was doting, and I was her little angel, whom she would protect when my dad would get drunk. I couldn't do anything to please my dad. And I couldn't do anything that my mom didn't think was just wonderful. My drawings were works of art, my room tidying was exemplary, my snow shoveling was so perfect that it made the angels sing.

So, in a weird kind of way, it didn't matter at all what I did, as this win-with-Mom-and-lose-with-Dad turned out to be a zero-sum game, though I sure liked winning with Mom a lot better.

And it was my mother who led me into my first encounter with the power of changing reality, through my art.

Good penmanship was important to people of my mother's generation, and she not only taught me art, but she taught me the same good penmanship, with those elegant cursive swoops, which were lighter on the rise and heavier on their descent than what we had learned as kids. They are kind of like the calligraphy that you see in the original Declaration of Independence. Hers was the penmanship learned by the previous generation to me, so, in other words, my penmanship matched that of my friends' parents.

That meant that I could and would write the notes-from-parents to present to the school office, explaining why my friends and I were not in class, inventing a reason other than "we were skipping out." Pretty soon, I had a small business going, charging a dollar apiece for these written excuses.

However, my friends and I were all missing so much school that our grades were slipping. That, in turn, presented another opportunity for me. I came up with a way to create a passable report card that I would sell to those who needed one for five dollars each.

My friends would show their parents the passing report card that I had designed, and then have me sign their real report card as their parent, with an added note that said the parent would see to it that their son would try harder.

This business went on for quite some time and I made a nice stash of cash, but inevitably the school's office called a parent about their kid's dismal report card, and the kid was pressured into ratting me out. The rest of that school year, my feet wore a virtual path to Principal Snow's office, who gave me a stern and rather biblical lecture on the dangers of bearing false witness (and who will return to my story later, in a most unexpected way).

I really connected with art in high school. The main reasons that I wanted to do excellent work in art class were twofold: I wanted to impress my girlfriend Susan who I was going steady with, and I wanted to make money.

My best friend Richie was a bit of a ladies-man in high school. His romantic plate was already full, so he set me up on a blind date with a girl who was impossible to ignore.

She was elegantly tall—what the magazines would call statuesque—with light-brown tresses. She was shapely and as creamy as a vanilla sundae. If there's such a thing as 'guilt-by-association', then there is also 'class-by-association'. Richie was a very classy guy, and it didn't hurt that I was his best friend.

Susan and my first date came off so well and we enjoyed each other's company so much that it seemed to have been orchestrated by the gods. So was the second. By the third date, we had become an item.

But we did have a fly swimming in our romantic ointment and that was Susan's father. Susan's father knew that he wasn't just blinded by parental bias in recognizing that Susan was no ordinary girl. More than just being pretty, she was poised, dignified and had a keen intellect. The world could be her oyster and he had forbidden his daughter to ever get involved with (1) an artist, (2) a theater major or (3) a writer. His solid Mormon sensibility had pegged all three as ego-centric, unrealistic and destined for failure. "Marry one of those and your life will be unhappy and will remain unfulfilled," he told her.

Looking back in hindsight, he probably hit the head of that nail with a titanium hammer, so I guess prejudices can save a lot of time and trouble. But he also knew that Susan was stubbornly determined in what she wanted so he tried not to make a huge issue out of me, to avoid igniting a fuse to her sense of rebelliousness.

So, I was going steady with Susan, and as I mentioned, I also wanted to get paid for my artwork. I would take Susan to Ogden's downtown and tell her that one day, she and I were going to design window displays, and make our names and our fortunes. Suddenly, I had real motivation to succeed because of teenage hormones and the almighty dollar.

I became really good friends with my art teacher, who saw that I had potential now that I had shown that I could "do" art. I became interested in graphic design in high school as well. I remember the teacher telling us that we were going to study hand lettering. I grew up during a time when Google was this annoying thing that clowns did with their eyes. They would make googly eyes. Lettering was something you did by hand, and it, too, was an art.

So, this teacher taught us hand lettering, which is a skill more than a talent. Anybody can learn to do it. I wanted to impress Susan, so I wrote her name in decorative, fancy hand lettering, and I knocked this teacher's socks off. He thought, "Wow, this kid's got some talent." But then he gave us some silly art assignments to follow up, and I thought that I needed a really good reason to motivate me. I didn't just want to get a good grade on an assignment. I wanted it to land someplace. And, as noted, I had two motivations: my girlfriend and money.

I went downtown to a high-end clothing store, The Blue Door. And I said to the owner, Wayne Wilcox, "Look, I've seen your window displays, and they look like the stuff the dog leaves on the pavement. Let me design posters that will attract attention and get people in your store. If you'll give me enough money for a date on the weekends, I'll hand it in as an assignment. And then I'll give it to you." He said sure, and so we had this thing going where I got to design his windows, he paid me $25, a small fortune at the time, and I got an A on the assignment.

The thing I learned with art was that I was going to need a reason to do it. I wasn't wired to sit down and just paint something to nourish my soul. I had to know why I was doing it. Call the "why" my inspiration. So, if someone was telling me that I had to do art to get a grade, that was not inspiration. That was an exercise. The Blue Door was doing art.

Learning hand lettering and making money from it was what got me interested in graphic design. When I needed money after high school, I did hand lettering and hand painted signs, getting gigs through word of mouth. Ironically, though it was not at all ironic at the time, I did the hand lettering on the Ogden sheriff and police cars.

In summer, I would go pick up the Sheriff cars, and drive them up and park them on the front lawn of my house. I remember driving a Sheriff's car and the guy driving in front of me slowed down to a crawl, as if going the normal speed limit would be an admission of all his crimes. So, I flicked on the siren in that Sheriff's car and the guy pulled right over. Expecting the worst. I gave him a jaunty smile and a wave as I drove past, and he looked stunned, his weather-beaten face saying, "I know that as you age cops keep looking younger, but this guy is a teenager!"

I would take those cop cars to my house, and with my tongue sticking out of the corner of my mouth—it's a thing that happens when I do art—and my lettering brush in hand, I would carefully paint the word "Sheriff" in black on the white Sheriff cars.

I would also do police cars, hand lettering "we serve we protect" in white on their black panels, in kind of a script. There were no decals in those days. Just the steady hand of Russ Swain letting people know who were the Sheriffs and who were the police.

After high school, I decided to pursue art as a major in college, at Ogden's hometown university of Weber State. My first year was kind of disappointing as I didn't really like the academic approach to art. Nuts and bolts is what I wanted to learn and not some solipsistic sort of approach which decreed that whatever's inside you, you just pull out and let it go. I wanted to be inspired to bring something from within me that I could reveal with sublime artistic technique.

My art courses were theoretical and practical. But even then, there was only so much I could do with a nude figure drawing. I mean, it wasn't as if I was going to have the people of Ogden lining up at my studio so I could draw them in their birthday suits. But if somebody said, "Hey, I want you to do a painting of my kid that will hang on the wall," then all of a sudden, you're reaching into a different level of your mind and your soul to say, "Well, I want to honor the relationship in this family with this kid, and I want to make it something that becomes a memory that they will treasure forever and the kid can look back on as an adult, and do the same for his child."

And then you've got the fact that when you're in college, you're distracted by girls, and I was certainly distracted by the females around me, and especially by Susan. My father used to tease me, saying, "By the time you graduate, you'll have to set aside 50% of everything you've learned in college, because you can't make a living from necking." I have to confess that I did try to make a living from it, and it did pay dividends that you couldn't spend in a shop, but even so.

I had my sights set on a bigger world, as I wanted to see what was out there beyond Ogden. I knew I would have that chance at the end of my first year of college, because I would take two years out of my studies to perform my mission for the Church of Jesus Christ of Latter-day Saints, aka the Mormons.

The mission, or the "calling" happens when a Mormon male turns 19. The church sends you a notice from the Prophet, who is the President of the Church, which reminds you that you are expected to serve the church's proselytizing efforts, and it tells you where you're going to do that, which could be anywhere on planet earth. The church, in its wisdom, was sending me to Brazil.

On the one hand, I thought, "Okay, that's great. I'll see a little bit of the world, maybe learn a foreign language or something." But deep down inside me, it was really challenging, because I had Susan, who I was really nuts about, mainly because she was and remained my first real girlfriend, and so I was walking that path of romance. Of course, her father wanted me to walk right off it, and he knew that I would eventually accept a mission call. He could bide his time until I would be called away for two years, at which time, he could wave farewell to me as Susan's interest diminished. I hoped it would not, but it was a chance I had to take.

Sure, I was comfortable in my little cocoon of existence, but I had a hankering to get out of Ogden. And my mother would be proud of me. I felt I had to honor my promise to the faith in which she had raised me.

So, the Mormon church in all its wisdom sent me a challenge by dispatching me to Brazil: the most Catholic country in the world! Since the Portuguese colonized Brazil in the 16th century, it has been overwhelmingly Catholic. And today Brazil has more Roman Catholics than any other country in the world—an estimated 123 million.

I shipped off to Brazil to serve my LDS mission, and suddenly found myself in the middle of the teeming city of São Paolo, with a population of just under seven million people in 1968. Or about one hundred times bigger than Ogden, Utah.

And Portuguese, the language of Brazil, swirled around me. I was like a deaf man at the opera, as I could see the action, but I couldn't understand a thing. I certainly had no understanding of this new place in which I'd landed. It was disorienting, and I felt completely lost. Which is what is supposed to happen when you go somewhere new and foreign but knowing it and feeling it are two different beasts, and I was feeling it in my bones.

To be sure, I'd gone through a two-month language training crash course, where I was taught to memorize some essential phrases, and some proselytizing dialogue. But to me, they sounded like passages from Beowulf being recited by cartoon mice.

I knew that in order to make it through my mission, I had to come up with a plan of action. So, from the first day that I arrived in Brazil, all thoughts of future fun or past attachments were severed from my consciousness. I locked into this perpetual present, designed to purge my soul of any trace of iniquity, impurity, or even individuality. I would deal with what was in front of me, day by day, and eventually, two years would be up, and I would be back home.

When you go on a mission, it's a highly structured process which I imagine is like what you might experience in the military. You live with families who put you up in their homes. Each day you rise at 6 AM, and study scripture. Then you plan your lesson and are out the door by 9 AM to proclaim the word to the people around you through teaching and having meals together. In the evening, you do more teaching, and are back home by 10 PM.

You live with a companion missionary for about three months, and then they rotate you out. So, you're in a new country, but eight times in your two-year tour of duty, you get moved and matched with a new person to a new area of the country. I lived in São Paulo, and I also lived in the countryside, but it was São Paolo where I began my mission, and where it ended, and whose culture and people changed my life.

About a couple of months into my life in Brazil, I and my assigned companion Elder Richards, from Salt Lake City (you always call your companion Elder and their surname, even in private), had spent a long day doing our Mormon work. On top of that, we had been fasting and we had missed our evening meal. We were tired and lightheaded and on our way home, under a light rain that made the cobblestone streets especially slippery as we walked to our *pensão* that we shared with a family.

We had several more blocks to go when I grabbed Elder Richards' coat sleeve and pointed out a neighborhood bar. I said to him, "Let's just jump in here, sit down and grab some hot chocolate to recharge." In Brazil, neighborhood bars are like convenience stores. You can get a beer or a loaf of bread or a hot chocolate.

We ordered something warm and snagged two seats at a small table. The rain created a halo of light around the streetlamp which added to the cozy ambience of this open-air bar. As we sat there, a young Black man entered the bar. He was shirtless and shoeless and wearing only a pair of worn-out shorts, and he carried with him a bucket of crabs.

His objective was to sell the shop owner his crabs. We watched while the shirtless man thrust a stick into his bucket, which caused one of the crabs to grasp it with a claw-like pincher. And with the crab clinging to the stick, the man walked around while shouting in Portuguese that these crabs were all fresh.

And suddenly, it occurred to me that I could understand what he was saying. I had not been aware that the language barrier had slowly been dissolving, and that I was entering a new state of reality. I started to chuckle, along with a small crowd of patrons who were also amused by his impromptu one-man circus act.

As I felt more relaxed, my eyes turned to the glowing street lamp outside, and through the animated curtain of swirling raindrops, the halo around the lamp became the glowing white circle of life. My vision could have been caused by lack of food or by dehydration, so I turned my intention back to the performer and the small crowd that was now erupting in laughter.

The shirtless man took a bow and then shook hands with

a shop owner to show us that a transaction had been made. In that moment, I became acutely aware of my new reality, and how to see it. I was going to embrace and enjoy this cultural uniqueness that I never could have witnessed had I stayed at home. And I was seeing a life view from another cultural perspective which added to it and expanded my own narrow vision.

And from that moment, I relished everything that was different from my American way of life. Whether the experience deepened my commitment to my faith is beside the point. It deepened my commitment to life. I was so busy with the duties of my mission and had so little time to myself that I did not do any art while I was in Brazil. But I did write to Susan whenever I could.

We corresponded weekly, the first year that I was in Brazil. During the second year, her letter writing became more sporadic. Near the end of the second year, she let me know she had begun dating other men but would still like to see me when I returned.

So, after two years in Brazil, experiencing the cosmopolitan life of the big city and seeing the simple pleasures of the countryside, I came home ready to take on the world, and to reconnect with Susan, and maybe renew what we had. I would also get my next shot at glory which I would make from Brigham Young University in Provo, Utah. It was much bigger than Weber State in Ogden, where I had begun my college art studies, and I had been preparing for this. I simply had to be resourceful, adaptable and stoic. I was more seasoned now, as a human. I had experienced the cosmopolitan life of a foreign country. I would be fine. I just needed a distraction.

BYU offered me a sense of community, and more dating opportunities now that Susan and I were finished, though I was not really. The beauty of a woman is not just a quality of face and skin but also of light. And that luster that had once shone so brightly for me, in her eyes, had dimmed. I no longer saw myself reflecting in them. There didn't have to be an explanation. I wouldn't make any vain attempts at trying to make it work. That would be madness. I simply stated, "You must follow your heart. I love you. Goodbye."

I thought of my father's adage, that "a guy can scratch most any place that itches, but he can't scratch his heart. Nothing can heal the sting of a woman."

So, while BYU had excellent academic programs, Susan's departure had torn a hole in the fabric of the deepest part of my being. As Mike Tyson famously said, "Everyone feels prepared until he's punched in the face." I wasn't ready for BYU. I had been accepted, but my landing there felt like playing a game of Emotional Musical Chairs. My young heart had a warp in it. I felt isolated—alien. When I applied to transfer in as a sophomore, I thought it would give me access to a wider world. To the work of Michelangelo and Picasso, and the thinking of Socrates and Shakespeare. But now there was an abiding emptiness. More than ever, I was missing the affection of my own family. So, by the end of the second semester, I packed my bags and returned home. And I went back to Weber State to finish my degree.

When it came time to leave college and go out into the world, I began my next chapter as a counterfeiter. I had to steal with both hands. I had written notes to my high school authorities pretending to be the parent of the note bearer. I loved doing that, and I made some money. Now I counterfeited a postage stamp to get that job with the advertising agency, and I did. I worked at the agency for a couple of years, got married, and started a family.

Then I started my own design and printing business. I opened Para Graphics in a little commercial strip mall, in Riverdale, and we were smack in the middle of the mall. I had a front office for customers, which I kept very tidy and welcoming. It had bookshelves—though no books on counterfeiting—and a comfortable couch. There were blinds on the windows to let me adjust the light as needed, or to put the place into total darkness.

The back of my shop was where the magic happened, with its printing presses and collating machine, and tables with stacks of paper piled up on them, and my darkroom.

I started Para Graphics with dreams of achieving big success. From my college brochure success. I could see myself designing posters for museums and events, like David Lance Goines. And those college brochure dreams got squashed by a racist college president, and I owed Tommy the Shark that chunk of money which started me on my next adventure in changing my reality. My new counterfeit project was going to be big, and it was going to change my life. It would certainly do that. And though I didn't know it at the time, I would decorate it all with the diamond dust which would make it work. And it is that diamond dust, which, in its way, has swirled around me ever since.

3

How to Make the Fake

On the day that I realized that I needed to make some money, as in manufacture it, my wife had just driven off early in the morning with our two daughters to meet her parents, who had returned to live in their native Utah from Hawaii, along with her aunts and uncles at a big weeklong family reunion. I had regrettably said no, I couldn't go with them on this great summertime adventure because I had too many work-related responsibilities. I needed to finish that big college brochure contract and so on. I had always tried to insulate my family from the financial pressures that I was under, and I did it again here, crossing my fingers that if my money-making plan worked, we would all be just fine, if not even better than that, and no one would be the wiser as to what I had done.

You might wonder if I had any doubts about what I was going to do. Not in the least. My only concern was pulling off my counterfeit $20 with such panache that my ruse would never be discovered, and I could live happily ever after. It worked with the postage stamp, and years before on my forged letters from the parents of absent pals —which were a kind of art—and I just needed it to work to pay off Tommy the Shark. That was my vision of success.

I didn't know it at the time, but I have since discovered that the U.S. government has a website with an article on how counterfeiting of money is done. The abstract of the piece, published in 1979 (so I could have used it back then) says: "banknote counterfeiting takes place in several stages: (1) the acquisition of appropriate paper, (2) the rendering of watermarks (often left out), (3) the reproduction of security marks, (4) the actual imprinting (today most frequently through offset techniques) and numbering of bills."

I had a printing press, along with the ink, and I had the right paper, which was critical. I had reams of paper from Crane's, who had been making currency paper for the U.S. government since 1879 when they beat out another company with a bid of 38.9 cents per pound of paper. Crane's developed a new paper, and by the end of the century, Crane's had tripled the life expectancy of one-dollar bills and more than tripled the tonnage they shipped to Washington, D.C

I had a few reams of Crane's paper because it was great for printing brochures. It wasn't exactly the same as the paper used by the U.S. Treasury Department, as their paper had silk in it, and mine was 100% cotton, but it was free of wood pulp, and felt enough like currency paper that I knew all I had to do was get the color right. Along with a few other things.

First, I had to stop any customers from walking in on me as I was creating my new financial reality. I had to draw the blinds on my shop, and to stop anyone who didn't read that signal, I hung out a sign that said, "I'm on vacation this week, but we'll be back in town on Monday." It was summer, and so, why wouldn't I be on vacation?

I also had to be discreet, as one of my clients, Morris Travel, was my next-door neighbor in the strip mall. They were great people, and great for business as I printed out their travel flyers, but they weren't going to generate enough cash for me to pay back Tommy. So, with my "gone on vacation" sign on the door, I could not let them see me coming and going into the shop without them asking why I was there if I was not supposed to be there. Mr. Morris also had a habit of dropping in to shoot the breeze a bit, which I always enjoyed, but which I could not afford to do while I was making my money. So, I had to arrive in the shop early, before Morris Travel opened up, and to stay long after they had closed, and to make sure that in between it looked as if no one was there. So that's what I would do.

It did occur to me that Tommy the Shark might stop by to look in on me, but then I dismissed that idea, as there was no beer and no almost naked dancing girls in Para Graphics. He would summon me to meet him when my time to pay up was on the calendar, and I would be ready.

I let the answering machine take care of all phone calls, and I checked all my messages, filing the "to do's" for when I was done. I tried to at least keep my finger on the pulse of the business, but I didn't want anybody to have a reason to need me urgently for anything and show up in a panic. As far as the world beyond my shop knew, I wasn't there.

But oh yes, I was there, from dawn until midnight, fueled by peanut butter sandwiches and gallons of milk, as I set out to use everything I knew about graphic design, along with some inspired guesswork, to create my money. There was no Mr. Google then to ask how to do it. I would have to create my counterfeit money from my own talent and resources. I would have to teach myself how to make the fake money.

The U.S. Treasury had recently issued new $20 bills that were supposedly harder to counterfeit, so I carefully studied the new bill with a jeweler's magnifying loupe. I looked at the way I would look at a piece of art. The man whose face adorns the $20 is Andrew Jackson, the seventh president of the United States. He was not going to be tough to reproduce. The hand lettering was something I could do as well. After all, I had hand-lettered the cop cars of Ogden.

I just needed to get the colors right, and the texture right, and find a way to reproduce those red and blue fibers that I saw through the jeweler's loupe. They were going to be tricky.

"Rag paper", which just means that it was 100% cotton, and that it was pure white, would be my base. That white slate would allow for more luminosity when I printed the full-bleed background color of the bills, knowing that the black ink overprint would reduce the amount of light reflected back. I thought that this luminous white paper was a good omen.

I mixed the inks. I started with a little pinch of yellow and the tiniest drop of black that made that yellow go a muddy green, to make the paper look like U.S. currency paper. This would allow me to do my next bit of counterfeiting magic.

Hand drawing the bill would not do. A photograph would give more objective detail. I was going to photograph it, and from there make my own adjustments. I was going to photograph it, and from there make my own adjustments.

I had put the crisp, new $20 bill under the lens of my graphic camera, and then magnified it by 400% and photographed it. That way I could clean-up any noticeable detail imperfections and separate the parts that would need to be omitted on the black plate, which prints those things that are black, and removing the serial numbers and treasury seal. Those would be printed on a separate pass through the press with a mix of green ink.

John, the guy who had introduced me to my wife, and who was a magician when it came to printing, had sold me my single-color, offset press. John could sense how the slightest variations of roller pressure would affect the amount of ink hitting the paper. He truly brought his craft to an art form, but running a business wasn't part of John's artistry, so he sold me his press and went to work for a large printing outfit where he could focus on what he did best.

I turned my attention back to red and blue fibers running through it, the ones that were barely noticeable to me when I spotted them with my jeweler's loupe, but which were essential. I would have to print those as well if I wanted to pass off my creation as the real thing, and I knew I was very close to pulling that off.

But those fibers were a problem. How could I get red and blue fibers into my bills? The question had been swirling around inside my head, and then, late one night, the answer whacked me in that head. The solution was right under my feet.

I had this little piece of black carpet in my darkroom, so I pulled the fibers out of it and laid them under the camera. I shrunk the fibers down to 25% so they looked like minuscule hairs. I photographed them, and then printed a red pass over them. Then I flipped my negative upside down, so that the same exact shapes are identical on the bill, and then I printed over them with blue. I had my background paper, and I had my red and blue fibers. And now, I realized that I had a masterpiece by the tail. In just one try.

There was, however, more to do. A lot more.

I had to give the Feds credit. They had designed a bill that was nearly impossible to duplicate! But I was determined to keep going because, so far, so good.

One of my challenges was that the offset press I was using was no match for the precision quality of gravure printing that the Feds used. Gravure printing puts an acid-etched image on the surface of a metal cylinder, and it uses one cylinder for each color in the print.

When you work the press, the engraved cylinder gets partially immersed in the ink tray, which fills its recessed cells. As the cylinder rotates, it draws excess ink onto its surface and into the cells. A "doctor" blade scrapes the cylinder before it touches the paper, so that the excess ink doesn't touch the areas not being printed, and which leaves the right amount of ink in the cell.

Since each cell on the cylinder has a different depth, this affects how you see the ink that the prints on the paper. The deeper cells produce more intensive color than shallow cells, and that was what was causing me problems now.

Try as I may, I couldn't hold that tiny white dot that appears in the shadow areas behind President Jackson's portrait. Not unless I could find a way to blow it out by upping the light on the exposure scale.

But when I did that, this then destroyed the tiny black dots that needed to stay in the highlight area.

I solved that problem by using a red tape masking trick known as rubylith to mask off areas on Andrew Jackson's face so that they couldn't get hit with light when I exposed it. Rubylith is two sheets of paper: the backing, which is clear, and the top, which is transparent and red. You used it to help change the light that hit images in graphic design, so that is what I did.

Then I removed the rubylith mask and shot Jackson's face again with less light so that those areas would be under-exposed. It worked. Those tiny black dots stayed. I was elated.

But new problems kept appearing, taunting me, and challenging me to solve them. I would run some sheets of paper through the press with my setup and then I'd make ready the green plate to print the treasury seal and serial numbers.

The problem was that there was no way to photograph them without either one of them muddying the waters. So, I thought well, there's a faster way that uses my lettering skills, so I just inked in the Treasury seal, and that other seal that says "Federal Reserve" by hand.

I also had to carefully hand-letter the serial numbers on the bills as well, since I didn't own a numbering machine, and I didn't have the means to buy one. I was pretty convinced that I probably could not find a numbering machine that would use that same typeface as the Feds used. I also figured that I could get by without one, as this was not my life's work. It was to get out of a jam, and then I would be done as a counterfeiter.

Since I could only run six bills on the size of paper on which I was printing, I had to hand-letter six separate serial numbers on each piece of paper on which the six bills would be printed. That meant that I would be limited to never spending more than six bills at a time, if I didn't want to risk some eagle-eyed soul spotting the same serial numbers on bills. Being spotted like that was unlikely, as who looks at serial numbers except cops and collectors, but I did not want to take that chance.

I was zeroing in on success and I knew that I was really close. What else could I be missing? The amount of time that I was putting into this project was exhausting, as I would wake up early, work until late, and dream of my creation while sleeping.

At the same time, it was incredibly stimulating, so I just kept pushing forward, asking myself "What am I missing?"

Memory helped me out. An acquaintance who was a blackjack dealer in Vegas once told me that the bills he took into his casino were dropped into a chute and then fanned-out on a table where they were exposed to black light. If a bill glowed, it meant it was counterfeit.

That meant that I had to find a way to block the effects of ultraviolet light to keep my bills from glowing in the dark under black light. I solved that problem by overprinting all the sheets of paper with a dead-flat varnish, which is a graphic design technique we use.

If you're printing something that is solid black with white letters on it, such as a book cover, you want to put a dead flat varnish on it so that fingerprints don't show. So, I thought all right, there's no sheen on money. So, I would put a dead flat varnish on the bills.

Since the varnish is oil-based, I mixed in a little high UV suntan oil to further block the effects of the ultraviolet detectors, and then ran it all through the printing press. I had an ultraviolet light in my shop and switched it on, and to that light, these bills looked like the real thing.

I don't know what drove me to zero-in on all these details. Had I been so detail driven when I painted my fake postage stamp? Was it fear driven? Was I going to have to sit again at the strip club with Tommy instead of watching the dancers wiggle and shake, and instead watch the sociopath Rhino come to shake me down for 10K? Was it greed? Was it my OCD compulsion? I don't know. Probably a mix of them all. I knew that I was so close to success. I had come so far, and I almost had it. But there was still this one last hurdle that I had to overcome.

That's when the buzzer on my shop door rang late one night. I stopped dead in my tracks. Who was out there just before midnight wanting to see me? Then a voice told me.

"This is the police. Open up or we're coming in."

My heart collided with my mouth. How could the cops know about my counterfeiting? I hadn't taken a single bill out of the shop. But now, I threw a tarp over the printing press, and grabbed a dummy brochure that I had made for the college that had fired me, and I hollered back:

"Hang on, I'm opening the door."

Standing on the other side of it were two Ogden cops, and I smiled as one of them I had known when I was lettering their police cars a decade or so earlier. If only I could remember his name. He remembered mine.

"Everything OK, Russ?" he said, while his partner had his hand on his holster, as if he'd draw and shoot me if I gave him the slightest reason.

"Well, no," I said. "Officer Watson." His name had just

popped into my head, and I turned up the wattage on my smile. "I had to put that sign on my door saying I had gone on vacation when I was actually stuck here, trying to finish this darn brochure."

I held it up so they could see it.

"That's interesting, Russ. Looks like a good college." Officer Watson said.

His partner's expression was of the kind I thought the college president might have had when he saw an Asian man and an African American woman on the cover. He looked like he had just sucked a lemon.

"Thanks, Officer Watson," I replied. "I have to get them a model of it by tomorrow, and so that's why I'm here so late."

He nodded. "When we saw the light coming from inside and saw the sign on the door saying you were on vacation, we thought there might be criminals in here."

I smiled again, but my heart was pounding. "No criminals. Just me. Trying to decorate our world a little bit."

He bid me good night, and good luck. Then I watched the two cops get into a car that I had probably hand lettered and drive off into the night.

As soon as they were gone, I ran back inside the shop, and with black duct tape in hand, taped every crevice that could emit light. I had been given a warning. With a big glass of milk and some oatmeal cookies, I calmed my nerves. Then I went back to work.

Visually, the bills looked excellent. When I held one that the Feds had made next to one of mine, I could not tell the difference, and believe me, I wanted to find anything that could expose my work as counterfeit. But they looked like the real thing.

What did they feel like in my hand? You can always tell when you're rummaging through a coat pocket, and you touch a bill. It feels different from a receipt or any other piece of paper. That's because the amount of pressure applied to the kind of ink during the engraving process makes it feel that way. The ink pressure creates a rough texture that feels almost like fine sandpaper, and when I put my bills in my pockets, my ink didn't feel like anything. It was just smooth to the touch and did not say "You are touching money."

I had been putting stuff into the ink mix to try to grit it up, and it had not worked. I wondered what could I use to give the ink a slight amount of textural feel without gumming-up the press?

The press had a powder-coating apparatus that could be set up to blow a very fine chalky powder substance onto the surface of each sheet as it ran through the press. It dried on contact and kept the printed sheets from offsetting onto each other as they came through the press. But it was fine as baby powder and pure white. Mixing that with ink would affect the color and not add any roughness.

Suddenly, I remembered my friend Felecia, who owned a small local jewelry store. She was a tall, dark haired voluptuous and attractive woman who was incredibly aggressive as a businessperson and always kept me a little off balance. But she had been my client, as we had been printing her ad flyers since we opened our shop.

She provided an array of services like clock and watch repair, gem polishing, as well as selling fine jewelry. We once printed a flyer for her with the headline, "Get Your Grandfather Fixed!" With a picture of a grandfather clock beneath it.

Felecia also offered free ring polishing. People came from all over to have their wedding rings cleaned and polished. She owned a machine that she used to polish jewelry. It had a small vacuum attachment that would remove very tiny particles of gold and diamond from a ring and suck it into a bag. Every few months she would filter and separate the fine particles of gold dust from that of the diamonds. She would keep and use the gold in mending cracks and fissures in gold rings. The dust from the diamonds she would eventually toss.

So, I called her. I asked if she still had any of that "diamond particulate stuff" hanging around. To my amazement, she told me that she did. "Why in the world would you want any of that?" she asked. "Just save me some! I replied. "I'm gonna tease my wife when she gets home from her trip. She's always wanted a full carat diamond. I want about ten carats' worth that I can put in front of her and say, 'Here, build your own!' "

Felecia just laughed and said that I could have her entire supply! So, I drove over to her shop in Ogden, which was about five miles away from my shop in Riverdale, and she handed me a bag of diamond dust.

I came back to my shop and mixed those tiny particles of diamond dust into the ink. They were very small, yet very hard. They didn't gum-up any mechanism because they were as fine as dust. But they created a very sand-papery feel to the ink. It was perfect.

I had created a $20 bill that looked and felt like the real thing. And as I had a few reams of Crane's paper, at 500 sheets per ream, I wound up printing about $250,000 worth of counterfeit $20 bills.

I had also burned a fair share of bills that didn't make the cut. I would have been smarter to go out in the woods to build a fire, but time was a crucial element. So, I thought that since my wife's family were out of town with her, and they had a wood burning stove in their basement, that I would use it. I had never worked on a wood burning stove, so I didn't know about flues. I just tossed in my dud bills onto the fire, saw them burning, then shut the door and said to myself, "That'll take care of itself. It'll all burn up."

Today, I've got a burn barrel out in my backyard to torch boxes and cardboard and stuff that I don't want to put in my garbage can. I just light them on fire and it burns to ash. It doesn't do that in a wood burning stove unless it's got the flue open so the smoke can get out. But I didn't know any of that. And at the time, I didn't know I didn't know, but I would come to find out that I had missed a very important detail.

Now that I had cranked out all the very fine looking U.S. currency, I need to stash it. I didn't have a safe, and besides, plunking one down suddenly in my shop would be asking for questions I didn't want to answer.

So, I put the counterfeit bills in the boxes that we used for business cards, as about a hundred bills fit perfectly into a box. I filled up the boxes and put them up on the shelf. Nobody ever wants to go look at what's inside of a box of business cards. Business cards are pretty boring, and I figured my small fortune was safe within them.

There was one more thing to do. I wanted to make the bills that I was going to test in the real world look like they had been in circulation, so I shoved them into the bottom of my shoes, and I walked around on them to give them that well-traveled feel.

And then I had to do that very thing I had created the bills to do. I needed to try out my creation. It would work, or I would go to prison. I was elated and afraid, but I had crossed the Rubicon a long time ago. I was going full tilt ahead, come what may.

I had made a $20 bill that I believed was real. I had used my artistry to convince myself, a kind of con artistry in reverse. But I knew that as I took my next step forward, I had become a counterfeiter. Now I needed to see if the world could see with me, or see through me.

4

How to Spend
Fake Money

The word "counterfeit" has an interesting etymology. In Middle English it appears as a verb from the Anglo-Norman French *countrefeter*, which in turn comes from the Old French *contrefait*, which is the past participle of *contrefaire*. And it comes from Latin with the *contra-* 'in opposition' added to *facere*—'to make.'

"In opposition to make." It's an interesting idea because reality is at the very heart of the matter. "In opposition" is a type of reality, and "to make" is another type. Was I opposed to the thing that I had made? Far from it. I was very much in favor. Was it in opposition to anything? Well, only to those other $20 bills that were already out there.

I had to test it to see if my $20 could join the larger family of $20s that was out there in the world, or if it would be rejected as "in opposition."

My \$20 bills looked amazing. Everything from the portrait of President Andrew Jackson to the color of the bill to the grit of the paper—thanks to the diamond dust I had used in the ink, from those shavings left over from expensive diamonds as they were shaped into ring stones—looked as though the bills had been pumped out by the U.S. Bureau of Printing and Engraving itself.

The only thing that wasn't so much wrong as it was limited were the serial numbers. I didn't have a numbering machine and so I had to duplicate serial numbers. That was going to work out just fine, if I was careful.

And I was going to be careful because I was scared to death.

I was a God-fearing Mormon guy who had never committed any illegal acts in my life, at least, not so far. I was a loving husband to my wife and a devoted father to my daughters. I went to church and the bishop liked me. I had gone on a mission to Brazil to proclaim my faith to others. And at its most basic level, I believed in right and wrong.

I also believed that what I had done was not wrong, but necessary. I had done it so that I could keep doing the right thing for my family. The wrong was canceled out by the right, or so I told myself.

As an artist, one is always subject to one's artistic impulses, as though you're channeling a creative energy. But now you have to put the full ray of your faintly ingenious skill against all the rules. As the painter Delacroix said, "There are no rules for great souls. Rules are only for people with mediocre talent."

That sounded good to me, for the time being. I wasn't going to be counterfeiting money for the rest of my life. That's why I hadn't bought a numbering machine. I was just going to do it until I got back on my feet, in terms of my business. Tommy the Shark would be summoning me soon to repay him, and if I could not, I wondered if he would send Rhino after me? Just for fun?

I had to prevent that possibility from happening. So now the question that I was asking myself was where could I spend a few of my $20s in a low-key way so that if anything went wrong, I could claim innocence? If I was questioned, I could say that someone must have given me a bad bill. But I didn't think that was going to happen because I knew that these were not bad bills. They were, in their way, Russ Swain masterpieces.

I had the stomach and the talent to make them. Did I have the stomach and the smarts to spend them?

There's a saying: think globally, act locally. I was thinking globally in the sense that I was thinking about how good our lives could be if I got us out of the hole we were in because of that canceled contract. We were in the hole because I had tried to do a good thing with the brochures I was printing for that college. My mistake was thinking that the colleges wanted Black and Asian people in their brochure. I was thinking globally, and the college canceled my contract because they were thinking like small-minded bigots. To put it politely.

I was also thinking locally about how I would try out my counterfeit twenties. I didn't want to go to a diner or anything, because I didn't want to linger. I didn't want to buy anything high end, which would cost me seven bills, because then I would be exposing the duplicate serial numbers. I had to keep it simple, and get in, then get out.

The local drugstore seemed like the perfect spot because it did a lot of business. Yet it wasn't in the business of suspecting its customers were going to try to pass them money that wasn't really issued by the government, but by Russ Swain.

Of course, on my journey to this point, I had asked myself "What is real money?" On the surface, it's just paper and ink. However, money issued by the government is "legal tender." Legal tender means all coins and currency that are minted by the government can be used in paying off debts—

as in, I want a soda you are selling, and my debt to you is the price of the soda. Interestingly, businesses don't have to accept coins and cash as legal tender. They can have debt repaid however they like. In gold coins, in hard boiled eggs, or in milk and cookies.

And in that idea, my mind opened up to thinking about how and what we use as money, and how inherently fragile the idea of it is.

Consider the Yapese people, who live on the Yap islands in Micronesia. They used stones, with holes bored in the center, as their currency. They would hand over a stone and take goods or service in return. The stones were worth something because the Yap believed they were worth something. Even if a stone fell into the sea and you couldn't see it, let alone use it, it was still considered worth something, just like gold from European ships that sank in the oceans hundreds of years ago still attract treasure hunters. Because they, and we, believe that shiny metal is worth something. Today, you can even exchange Yap currency for U.S. dollars. One thousand Yap stones today are worth, in the minds of currency exchanges, $2.42 cents.

In the Middle Ages, people in England paid their rent with eels, because landlords wanted eels. There was a religious connection that helped make this payment method attractive as well.

In Catholic monasteries and religious institutions before the Reformation, the eel was also money. There were many days on the Catholic calendar in which you had to abstain from meat, particularly during the forty days of Lent before Easter. Meat markets shut down, and fish was the primary product, so monasteries saw eels as a high demand commodity and collected them in massive amounts from their tenants as payment.

The point is, anything can be money if you think it has value.

I wasn't trying to exchange stones or eels at this drug

store. I was going to give them paper money that I had made, and I had to thank China for that invention. Paper currency was first used in the Song dynasty which began in the 10th century CE. When Marco Polo went to China in the 13th century CE, he was amazed to see these pieces of paper in circulation that had great value to the locals. You could buy silk or noodles or women or opium with the paper. It's even in the book that he wrote about his travels, in a chapter called "How the Great Kaan Causeth the Bark of Trees, Made Into Something Like Paper, to Pass for Money All Over his Country." And with that, Marco had attracted the attention of Europe's money people.

By the middle of the 17th century, Europe was using paper money, too. The paper money was tied to gold, with the idea being that you could exchange the paper money's declared value for the same amount of gold. Which gave people faith that the paper was worth something because the shiny metal was worth something. And who of course tied the paper to gold? The government: which at the time was the royal treasurer. Their gold, their money.

The United States "greenback," which was what I had counterfeited, had come into existence in March 1863, created by President Lincoln's government to help finance the Civil War.

The colors, designs, serial number, signatures, and borders were designed to limit counterfeiting, which had been easy to do with bills called Continentals, which were issued during the American Revolution. With the help of the newly formed Secret Service, counterfeiting was kept under control. I will introduce you to the Secret Service a bit later, doing that very thing.

In the 1970s, the U.S. paper money, which was still backed by gold, went off what became called the "gold standard" and then, so did most everyone else. Money was subsequently worth something because the government allowed us to pay taxes with it, which pretty much sums it all up today. Crypto will be a serious currency once Uncle Sam says you can pay tax with it. Until then, it's an idea in the ether. Yap stones have more basis in monetary reality.

It is that fact right there that gives us a key insight into money. It's whatever we think it is. If I look at a piece of paper that says it is worth $20, what does that mean? What is $20? It is the three Starbucks White Chocolate Creme Frappuccino Grandes which run $5.75 each plus tip. It's 6.8 trips on the New York City subway. It's the price of a book, like this one.

It is based on our belief that this piece of paper is worth whatever we think twenty dollars is worth. We believe that handing it over will satisfy that condition, and I can walk away with twenty dollars' worth of goods. Or the change from twenty dollars' worth of goods, as that was my plan. I needed to launder my own counterfeit money, so I needed change from the $20 to clean up my crime.

The drugstore I chose was one on the other side of town. I did not want anyone I knew to bump into me. It was a mom-and-pop kind of shop that was not busy when I entered, but I was busy.

My nerves were screaming at me, sweat was glistening on my brow and my heart was pounding as if I had been chased down a dark alley by the Money Police, along with Tommy and Rhino and my wife and her family and everyone in my church, who were all about to give me a thrashing for my sins.

I needed to calm down, but I could not. I had every confidence that my counterfeit money would pass, but I would not know if that confidence was well placed or downright crazy until I spent it.

I looked at the woman at the cash register, who was a little older than me, and I was in my early thirties. She looked kind, and as if she had a family and a life and was trying to make her ends meet by working here. I had to somehow use that, and my own state of near panic, to pull off my test.

I looked around the drugstore. What could I buy to cover the fact that I was so nervous? Vitamins? No. Cold and flu remedies? No. Tampons. Yes!

I would buy a box of tampons to see if the money worked, and to cover my own sweaty trembling self.

I picked up a box and walked up to the cashier, who looked at sweating, nervous me and immediately her face turned to one of maternal concern. "Are you OK?" she asked.

It was my cue. "I'm just not used to buying these..." I said, gesturing to the box. "I guess it affects my nerves."

She gave me the kindest smile and told me not to worry at all. "Guys buy these for their wives and girlfriends all the time," she said, trying to buck me up as a doer of a good. I gave her a shy smile in return, and then I handed her my first fake $20.

Would she spot something I missed? Would she tell me to wait and then go to the back room and return with a guy holding a baseball bat who was going to give me a beating? No, she just took the bill and put it in the cash register and gave me the change.

It was the moment that changed everything.

When someone gives us money, we don't think the money is fake. We just think it's worth what it says it is worth, and that's exactly what she did. That's exactly what everyone did as I went around town for the next couple of days, buying boxes of tampons and washing my twenties. By the time I was done, I had a couple of thousand dollars in washed money and a couple of dozen boxes of tampons, as well as other small items I had bought.

When my wife and our daughters returned from their vacation, I was delighted to see them. Of course, part of me wanted to tell them how clever I had been while they were away, but a stronger part of me said that this was a secret to carry to my grave. Or to prison. Whichever came first.

When my wife went into our bedroom to unpack from her vacation, her eyes popped at all these boxes of tampons stacked in our bedroom closet as proof of my triumph—of which she knew absolutely nothing.

Of course, she wanted to know why this glut of tampons was there, and I had an answer. I told her that once she had made me go buy tampons for her in the middle of the night. As I did not want to repeat that experience, I took the initiative to make sure that she was well stocked for the foreseeable future. And that she had more than enough to share with her friends, even.

My wife, the soul of goodness, and a very devout woman, immediately apologized to me for clearly creating such trauma to my psyche that I had to do this. But she accepted my version of events, and I was relieved. I took no enjoyment in not sharing the full truth with her—which you might call lying, and yes, I would agree—but in my economy with the truth I was serving a higher economy, which was the well-being of our family. I truly felt that the end really did justify the means.

My next money laundering venture was to use the clean cash that I had gathered in my tampon buying to retrieve something my wife had given me, and which I needed to get my hands on before she noticed it was missing.

A couple of weeks prior to my decision to create my own currency, I had visited a pawn shop to secure a $200 float while I engaged in my creation of the brochure that was about to be canceled.

I had used the gold, ruby ring that my wife had given to me on the day we got married in order to secure the loan, and now that I had some cash, I was anxious to get it back before she noticed that I wasn't wearing it.

I returned to the pawn shop and presented the owner with my pawn ticket and a handful of banknotes to cover the balance. Half the notes were cleaned up currency I had gathered while buying tampons, while the other half consisted of the Russ Swain $20 bills. I thought, why the heck not? We were kind of in the same business, of determining what we thought was the true value of goods, and he might know better than anyone when he saw a fake.

The owner of the pawn shop, a gruff unsentimental guy who had seen everything, stood expressionless while he studied the bills that I had handed him. Then he took my ring from the glass showcase in which it had a position of prominence, but thank goodness, no buyers, and he laid it on the counter. Then he eyed me up and down, and barked, "Wait here!" Then he disappeared into the back room with the bills.

Alarm bells were ringing in my head. This pawn shop guy, who had seen all kinds of desperate people try desperate things, had made me. He had spotted my fake money. There was only one thing to do, and that was to get out of there fast, as the guy already had his money, and I had the ring.

I nervously grabbed my ring and headed briskly toward the door when the pawn shop owner emerged suddenly and yelled "Hey! STOP that guy!" His henchman-like partner, a muscle-bound enforcer, stepped in front of the doorway, blocking my escape. I stopped, and turned to face the owner, adjusting my voice to as nonchalant as I could make it with Big Trouble, in a few variations, staring me in the face.

"Is there some kind of problem here, sir?" I asked.

"Yeah!" he said, looking like he was going to kill me. "You got six dollars change coming!"

I let out a sigh that could've flattened a little pig's straw home as he handed me my six bucks. Then I strolled out of there with sweat running down my back, and a song in my heart. My $20 bills had not let me down.

I had made quite a lot of money, about $250,000 in fake twenties. I could not let my bills sit in my office and be neglected. Not when my family was around. But I could not risk spending the cash in Ogden, Utah. The tampon guy could not be seen spending his counterfeit bills on anything else that would attract attention. And Tommy was checking in on me regularly, almost as if he thought we were friends. I did not let him know that I could pay him back. I enjoyed making him think that I might not be able to do so because unless I got arrested in the next few days, I knew that I could.

I also knew that I needed to go to another state to spend my money. To the west was Nevada with the gambling dens of Reno and Las Vegas shimmering like temptation. I knew that casinos shone ultraviolet light on all their bills, and the fakes would glow in the dark because they hadn't been treated the way the government's bills had been. That would not be a problem, as I had found a way to block the effects of ultraviolet light to keep my bills from glowing in the dark under black light by overprinting all the sheets of paper with a dead-flat varnish, and I had tested it in my shop.

But now, I needed to test it out in the marketplace, to see if maybe my ultraviolet light was not the gold standard. Where could I go to properly test my $20s? There were ultraviolet lights in that stripper bar which Tommy liked to hang out in, but that was not an option. There was a sun tanning shop a couple of miles down the road, and even though it was summer, and even though I have pale skin that does not do well in the sun, I lathered on high-factor sun block and tested my $20s under the ultraviolet lights of a tanning salon. My $20s did not glow. They were as good as real to this tanning salon light.

So, now while I was confident that I could get in and out of Nevada, I rejected it as any kind of viable laundering option. There were too many professionals in those gambling dens on the lookout for the slightest tell that someone, like me, was up to something illegal, a tell that I might not even know I had. I would not be offering them that chance.

To the east was Colorado, and I didn't feel like trying my luck in big city Denver or college town Colorado Springs, with the Air Force Academy and all the keener airmen swanning around there, not exactly looking to take twenty-dollar bills from me. I needed a place full of kindness and trust. I needed farmers and potato fields as far as the eye could see, with a summer fairground parked close by where all the carnival buskers would love me and my money. I needed to go due north, to Idaho.

So, I told my lovely trusting wife that I wanted to take her to the delightful resort town of Sun Valley, Idaho for the long weekend. She was very happy to make the trip; she had missed me at the family reunion, and she did not want to let the summer slip past without us going away together. The girls were sorry to see us go, but glad to stay with my wife's parents and get spoiled a little. And so, my wife and I hopped in the car for our three-day adventure.

It's about a five-hour drive from Ogden to Sun Valley if you don't try to set land speed records, and I was all about stopping to spend money as we went. And every time we'd stop, I'd say to my wife that we had to get some gas. I would give her a fake $20 and ask her to pay the clerk inside while I pumped the gas. She went in, paid the bill, and came back with the change.

Or when we'd stop at a convenience store, I would use the restroom and give my wife another $20 and ask her to pick up some sodas. She would do it and give me the change. Did I feel like I was betraying her, and our marriage vows by having her launder money for me? No, I did not. I believed that I was providing for my family, and if I had insisted on buying everything from gas to groceries myself on our trip, that would have made her suspicious. As it stood, life was normal, or as normal as it could be with us laundering my counterfeit creations.

My pockets were heavy with change by this point, and I knew that I needed a faster, more aggressive way to clean my "dirty" money—again, just a matter of how you view cleanliness.

My wife liked to turn in early. We'd knock around Sun

Valley by day, walking the trails, and enjoying the mountain air, and getting in a full day of exercise and sightseeing. She would be done for the day by 10PM, and as soon as her head hit the pillow, she was safe in the arms of Morpheus.

That was my cue. I would tell her before she conked out that I still had a few more hours in me, and I was going to go see what was up at the local fairgrounds. If she didn't mind. She totally supported my journey to the wholesome activities of carnival-land, and away I went.

It was, if I may say so myself, a stroke of genius. The state fairgrounds are teeming with hawker and gawker, and they made a template for a guy like me with my newfound laundering game. At the fairground I found a collection of guys who wanted me to spend money, calling out to me as I passed by to come and try to win a stuffed bunny or bear, maybe worth 50 cents, far less than the fake twenty I would put down to try to win it.

I found considerable success with those amusement games where the workers try to tempt patrons into testing their skills for a buck. Most people stepped up and paid with smaller bills. Therefore, the carnival hustlers were more than happy to receive a large bill from me and unload the smaller ones to make more room in their cash box.

I walked casually up the row of amusement arcades where I let the hustlers descend upon me. One guy called out to me and said "Hey, you're tall, come and shoot some basketball." He was operating a stall where you see how many basketballs you could put through the hoop.

I said sure and asked him if he could break a $20 bill. He was happy to do that, because people had been giving him small bills all night, and he wanted to get rid of them. It was something like fifty cents or a buck per turn, so it was a small expenditure. I broke my $20, pocketed the change, and then missed most of my free throws. The last thing I wanted was to win back my $20!

I thanked him for the chance to show everyone how not

good I was at hoops, and we had a laugh, and I moved on. I told him my girl was waiting for me and we couldn't stay, and he immediately understood the urgency.

The next guy thought I looked like an athlete (clearly having not seen my basketball adventure).

"Oh, my man, look at you! Y'all a natural! I bet you can pitch a ball like nobody else!" he said, wanting me to chuck a rubber baseball at some aluminum milk bottles balanced on a bar stool.

"Dunno... I never played much ball," I said.

"Well, you come over here and let's see what you got!"

"Thanks, but I've only got a twenty. Besides, I gotta meet-up with my girl in ten minutes," I said, now enjoying the game.

"Then that gives you enough time to see if you are an athlete! Step-on-up here!"

I did the same with a water pistol shooting game, and a pellet shooting game, going up one side of the row and down the other. Each time I couldn't stay for another game because my girl was waiting for me.

I had to empty my pockets and stash the money in my car before I went back for more. I was thinking about what was going to happen to my $20s when the fair broke up and moved on. My bills were going to be disbursed all around the country. My work would be seen in states I had never visited! I felt a surge of pride at that.

And I also thought that I was doing these carneys, who work hard and have to put up with a lot, a good deed. I was helping them get rid of their small bills, taking their $1s and their $5s and their $10s and lightening their load. I was providing a public service on behalf of carnival workers.

On my first stroll through the park, I was wearing a pullover sweater and jeans. After I had stashed the cash that I had received under the seats of my car, I donned a light jacket, a baseball cap and removed my glasses and did the same thing all over again. No one recognized me from before because I got the same pitches from the same guys, who just wanted me to spend. I realized that if they weren't looking at their customers, they sure weren't going to be looking too hard at my money. I dropped the "my girlfriend is waiting for me" line and just ended each encounter with a yawn and a "it's been a long day" smile.

I wasn't tired at all, as I was running on adrenaline, but I didn't want to press my luck nor make myself look conspicuous. So, after a couple of runs on each side of the aisle (and back to the car again to unload) I decided to just amble through the crowd and play-it-by-ear. I stopped to buy some cotton candy, and then I saw another way to clean up my $20s.

Now cotton candy is not one of my favorite things in the world, and in fact, I think it might be the work of Satan himself, but it's a fairground staple and kids love to chomp down on all that ethereal sugar.

Taking care to only touch the wrapper of my cotton candy stick, I'd spot a young guy and say, "Here kid, you want this? I gotta find my girlfriend."

The kid would take the cotton candy eagerly, and I would walk to the next group of kids. I'd buy ride tickets and give them to any kid who was running low. I'd buy hot dogs and sodas and hand them out to the kids like I was some fairground Robin Hood.

If anyone might have seen my behavior as erratic, it was because I was feeling anxious to find my impatient girlfriend, and who can't relate to that? I was the fairground lover, and she was the one who wanted to push off to more interesting pastures, so I had the sympathy of everyone. They loved the fair, too, and saw me as a fellow traveler.

I was picking up currency by the bucketload. The pockets of my jeans and jacket were so engorged with cash that I felt that I might attract the suspicion of those paying any attention to me, so I would return to my car to unload. Making certain I wasn't being followed, I would again start stashing cash under the seats.

After doing this for a couple of nights at this little Idaho fair I had fetched a hefty return without raising an eyebrow. No cops or carnival barkers had twigged to what I was doing. And the kids loved me.

My nightly work at the fairground was simultaneously exhilarating and exhausting. It was exhausting, due to the fact that every night I had to wrestle the Angel of Guilt into submission. But by morning, I arose as though I'd been given a shot of courage by the Angel of Success!

I realized that in creating these counterfeit $20 bills, I had also tapped into my own creativity. I had now invented the game I needed to play to get a return on my counterfeit creation. My audience was no audience—I was looking for no reaction at all. That was my applause for a job well done. I was impressed with what I had accomplished, but I could not tell a soul. Especially not my lovely wife, who just thought I loved these little state fairs.

I was no longer the sweaty, trembling guy who was buying tampons to cover his fear of getting caught. Now I had proven to myself that I could put it all off on a larger stage, so to speak, and I wanted to test this new character who was emerging, this darker side of my fair-haired Mormon self.

So, I wandered around Sun Valley a bit and then went shopping, in order to gather new data for my enterprise. I bought a few random items—a magazine, a pair of sunglasses, a fancy necktie—starting small to see how things went. Then I started pushing the boundaries of this new game by buying higher ticket items like jewelry and clothes.

I would use two or three twenties with an array of smaller bills parked between them to use as a distraction when I paid for things. I soon learned that people don't study currency. They merely glance at the denomination and whichever President's face accompanies it and then stick it in the cash drawer. They accept that what you are giving them is genuine, because we are not trained to think that everyone might be a counterfeiter, unless you work in Vegas.

For the first time in my life, I was living large. I found an exclusive little jewelry store and bought a gold-chain necklace to give to my wife to thank her for all she had done, and what she did not know she had done. For myself, as a kind of congratulations, I bought slacks, new shoes, and a ninety-dollar polo shirt. I would lay down multiple bills, as long as they added up to more than the price tag of the item in question so I could pocket the change—always careful to watch not to deliver two bills with the same serial numbers to the vendors.

In the higher-end stores of Sun Valley, the places that sold jewelry and fancy clothing, I would ask if they had any larger bills that they could exchange for smaller ones, since they always needed small bills to make change. Of course, they always did, and my wallet was soon bulging with fifties and hundreds, while my pockets were stuffed with my fake twenties to spend.

I even stuffed my shoes with my fake twenties as I had done when I first minted them to make the bills look as if they had been in circulation a long time. And so, they were even more likely to be taken at face value, because they showed they had been handled by very many people.

Suddenly, I was wearing nicer clothes than the ones I had traveled to Sun Valley in. I had beefed up my entire wardrobe. I even had one of those little gold clips that hold your shirt collars down. I was eating in some fabulous restaurants—and each time I would praise my waiter for his service and give him a healthy tip. I could slow down now. I could get a decent haircut and leave another healthy tip. I would smile at everyone! This was America! I was rich!

My one last thing to do was address the thing that started this all off. I had to pay back Tommy the Shark the $10,000 I had borrowed from him, along with the 10% interest that had kicked in. I could afford the interest, as I would have more than enough twenties in business card boxes, and I would smile as I handed it over to him, while also thinking about how Tommy was a greater sinner than me.

The Bible is pretty clear on usury in many places, but my favorite is the Book of Ezekiel, Chapter 18, where all the bad things you should not do are listed, and the man who commits usury, who "lends at interest, and takes profit; shall he then live? He shall not live. He has done all these abominations; he shall surely die; his blood shall be upon himself."

The Bible says nothing at all about counterfeiting $20 bills.

As I mentioned earlier, Tommy the Shark wasn't some hulking muscle-bound hoodlum in a black leather coat, with who-knows-what? kind of weapons concealed within. He was the type of guy you wouldn't look at twice on the street. And he was a Mormon, like me, so we shared a culture and a faith and that was somewhat reassuring, even if Tommy had no real connection to the church anymore.

Even so, beneath his basic civility and ordinary guy-ness, he had a very distinct air of menace in his eyes, and he could transfer that to his tone of voice. When he called me to invite me to the club, his "How's it going Swain?" managed to convey that if I didn't repay him at his hefty rate of interest, he would find a painful way to make me do so.

He never said what that way would be, but the sharp daggers that could flash in his eyes suggested that it would hurt, and he was looking at me with those eyes and expecting my excuse as I met him in his "office" at the Happy Trails stripper bar.

I had planned for this moment with a spring in my step. When I was in Sun Valley, I was amassing a fairly large amount of mostly small bills, and I brought along a small canvas gym bag into which I stuffed them. I knew I needed to get $10,000 in pretty clean cash to pay Tommy back, as he was probably the kind of guy who would look at serial numbers.

And so, I thought while traveling with my wife, while I'm up here in Idaho, I'll stop in at a credit union. I had found that the creativity I had expressed at the fairground, the stories of "my girlfriend waiting for me" had unlocked all kinds of other stories I could tell. So, I just went into the credit union and told them that I was the band teacher at the local junior high school, and that we had done this big fundraising event because we were trying to pay for new band uniforms. I told the story as if I believed it, and so they believed me.

I explained to the credit union that as a result of our successful fundraising, I had amassed a small fortune in small bills that was giving me a supercharged migraine trying to keep track of them all. I wondered if I could exchange my small bills for larger ones. As in, me getting some $100 bills in return would be a wonderful outcome.

I made sure that I didn't overwhelm them by exchanging the entire amount—I did around five grand at one credit union, and smaller amounts at a couple of others—and I never said that I had an account with the financial institute in question. I just behaved as if I did, with my newfound swagger. I told them I didn't need to make any deposits yet, but that I needed cash for some expenses that the band had coming up. Who doesn't want to help the junior high school band teacher? And these credit unions were all very helpful.

So, I went to pay Tommy at the so-called gentlemen's club, the one-story windowless joint near the airport. I made sure that I was on time, and I put the $10,000 in a cigar box. It was filled with three stacks of $100 bills wrapped in plastic bands.

As for the interest that I owed, because I was paying back late, I slipped in some of my fake twenties into a separate envelope, along with some $50s. When I got to the gentlemen's club, I sat down opposite Tommy, keeping the cigar box close to me. He wasn't sure what I was doing with the cigars and was so puzzled by it that he told me he didn't smoke them at all.

I smiled and slipped the envelope across the table to him. He opened it, and counted the money and I said, "That's your interest." He immediately demanded, "Where is the rest?" He thought he was back in control, and that I did not have the rest.

I smiled again and said "It's in cash, in the cigar box. I just didn't think you'd want me to open a cigar box with $10,000 in cash in this place."

I slid the cigar box toward him, and he glanced inside. He could see three bands of $100 bills, and he looked at me and smiled. Not warmly, but smugly. Then he said, "You're alright, Swain."

Now it was my turn to observe Tommy in this stripper bar, to take control of the room. He honestly didn't believe that I was going to come through with the repayment, and he thought he was going to have to make me squirm. And I don't know if he was disappointed that he didn't have to do that or not. He never said it, but I liked to think he never said it because I had won.

Tommy gave me a clue when he asked, "So how did you do it, Swain?" He was clearly impressed, while also highly curious about how I had pulled it off. It was almost as if his brain was racing through files to recall any recent and local bank unsolved robberies.

"That cat is bagged, Tommy," I replied with complete pleasure in my power. "And I am not at liberty, at this time, to grant the cat amnesty."

He smiled and nodded and took the money and left. He didn't care where it came from, and it never occurred to this guy who was very smart, and very shrewd about money, that I had just handed him a thousand dollars in interest made up of fake bills, and the principal made up of money laundered from my fakes. He believed that I had repaid him with "real" money and so, in that belief, I had.

I was feeling very good about what I had accomplished. I was not sweaty or nervous or even tempted to watch the ladies dancing. I was, in a way, like Tommy. But then I was not, as I was self-made. I had dug myself out of that troublesome financial hole with my own resources, and frankly, with my talents. I was proud of the bills I had designed, and I had carefully looked at each one that came off my printing press to make sure it passed my muster. If it did, it went into a box that was made to hold business cards. If it did not, I would get rid of it through the power of fire at my in-law's place.

Even so, in my solitary moments reflecting on my new life of crime, I did not think our God in heaven's master plan for me was to be a professional counterfeiter. But that thought was always overridden by this exciting feeling that any second, something could happen. I was living large and living on the edge.

Every morning I would wake up, and my feet couldn't wait to hit the pavement. Sure, the money was nice, but there was another force in play. It was that rush of adrenaline that I would feel each day, a rush that gets profoundly addictive.

And I realized, in a way, that I was starting to get addicted to my own body chemistry. My own adrenaline shots juiced the excitement of doing my money laundry, because I craved that feeling that any second, something was going to happen when I spent my money. Was someone going to call me out? Was I going to get caught? Was Tommy going to bust through the door screaming I had cheated him with fake money? Would my wife go shopping and get busted with my cash? God forbid my kids would find out, or my in-laws.

With each transaction the answer to all of those questions was no, they won't, and no, I won't. I had never imagined that I would be a successful money forger, but that's what I was, and I had invented stories to help me clean up my money. People believed the reality I had presented them with. And so long as I kept the source of my proffered realties to myself and took care not to double up on serial numbers when buying, I would be fine.

Of course, I was right about all of that, because in the end, betraying my own instinct was what would lead to, well, not the end of my life of crime, but a change in my path. But not quite yet.

I also noticed that guilt had started to raise its voice when I was alone in the dark. Guilt is a feeling that's hard to get rid of when you're in the process of shedding your values. The deeper I progressed down this forbidden path, the more aware I became of the ghost looming on the darker recesses of my mind. He haunted me constantly with the same questions: "Do I like this version of myself? Is this who I really am at my core? Or is life just throwing me some kind of test?"

At the beginning, I felt this duality of my persona. There was the old me, true-hearted, full of purpose; and a secret, private me that justified any means to the end. As the two personas began to morph into one, I sometimes felt like I was no one at all.

Whenever I sought relief in solitude, the shadows grew deeper. I was justifying this new life path by reminding myself that the bills were being paid. I had responsibilities and I was taking care of them. But wherever I went, whether I was in a crowded restaurant, or alone on a desolate street in the inner city, that unfriendly ghost was there, dismantling every assurance that I tried to give myself that this was simply what I needed to do.

So now the ghost began reminding me what my true fear was. I feared the creature; the one that disturbed my slumbers, the creature that I was becoming—the creature that was hiding in that nameless darkness which was my own identity.

Now, as I reflect on these experiences, it brings me to the realization that they've left their marks on me, like scars, like cattle brands, like faded shore-leave tattoos. But at the time, I managed to put the ghost in a dark room at the back of my mind and get on with what I had created. After all, I was addicted to what I had created.

5

My Mexican Rocks

One of the most surprising things to me about my creation of the Russ Swain $20 is that it led to a friendship with Tommy the Shark, whose 10% a month vig was frighteningly steep—perhaps enforced by the fists of the sociopathic Rhino—and which had inspired me to become my own mint in the first place.

After I surprised Tommy by repaying him, he wanted to see more of me. I figured he was on to me and my "money making" business, and he wanted to know more, or maybe even go into business with me. I didn't know how he could have figured it out, but with success at counterfeiting comes a certain degree of what I call zealous caution, so I was nervous about what he might want, and I dodged him. I didn't want my wife and daughters to know about him and start asking me questions. If they knew about Tommy, they would know that I was, well, up to something on the dark side.

And my printer friend John had run into some darkness as well. He was having trouble with a new business that he had started and wanted to know if I wanted to buy him out.

The last thing I needed was to have two Para Graphics shops open now that I had my own humming along so nicely. I thought two would be tempting fate. But I didn't want to let my friend down. I told John that I would think about it, which I did, for a minute or so. And then I filed John and his problem in a remote and dingy corner of my mind and got on with figuring out what to do about Tommy the Shark.

I concluded that I had better see Tommy before he rolled into Para Graphics to see me, and even worse, be seen by my wife. We met at his usual spot, the Happy Trails strip club, and he began to open up to me a bit. He sipped a beer, and spoke softly, without his usual edge of menace. He didn't tell me his life story, or anything like that, but he did tell me that he was having some health issues. The doctors thought he had MS, but were running some more tests on him, and he needed to have some fun in the sun. So, he asked his milk-drinking Mormon counterfeiting buddy (which he did not know about yet) to go with him to his favorite place in the world, Mazatlán, Mexico. He would even pick up the tab.

I had not expected that the guy with the hard stare from his perch in the stripper bar would want to go on a sun holiday with me, but then I realized that I might be his only real friend. I was flush with my business card boxes of $20 bills, and business at Para Graphics had picked up, but I had everything in order at work. So, I felt that I could use a little away time and spread some of my money around Mexico.

I asked my wife if she minded that I go away with a Mormon friend for a bit of a holiday after all the work I had been doing, and she said that I deserved it. After all, I was not able to attend her family reunion with the girls, because I had been working, and she felt bad about that. I felt bad about that too, but I also knew that Tommy's gesture was about more than a trip to Mexico. I didn't know what, but I felt that he needed me to go, and my wife agreed that I should take some time off and let loose. So, I said yes to Tommy.

The farthest and only travel adventure I had was to Brazil, which was for reasons of religion, and in a way, I would learn, so too would this journey to Mexico be about a kind of faith. I had not been to Mazatlán before, but I could immediately understand why Tommy loved the place. Located about halfway down Mexico on the Pacific coast, the city is a popular tourist destination because of its wonderful beaches, and its splendid boardwalk out into the Pacific, and its cuisine, based on the local fishing industry. There's a historic old center that radiates Spanish, French and indigenous charm, all seasoned with a bit of Germany, as many Germans settled here in the 19th century, and contributed to the city's food and culture. You even get Mexican bands here that play polkas.

At the time we were there, in the mid-1980s, it was a city of a little under a quarter of a million people, so the population number matched the amount of money I had printed up. I thought that was a good omen.

Tommy, the strip club veteran, was much more of a hell-raiser than me. His idea of fun was spending nights hanging out in strip bars, drinking *cerveza*, and especially so with possible multiple sclerosis diagnosis pending. I had no interest in doing what we already did in Ogden at Happy Trails, but I accompanied him and his beer with my colas to a couple of places to be a good sport.

But I also felt that Tommy wanted more from me, maybe something like friendship. So, I needed to test that by telling Tommy as he was into his third beer one night the truth: that I had repaid him in part with counterfeit money. Money that I had made with my own hands.

He wasn't angry. He was interested, but not in having me make more fake money for him. No, it was a turning point of sorts where his respect for me transcended the fact I had repaid him at all. The fact that I had done this—that I had even done this illegal thing—to make good on my debt now rose to something like respect for me as a person. He had seen me first as an adversary and maybe as a threat, but now here in Mexico he really did see me as a friend. I had changed that reality, too.

But tonight, I needed to change my reality from yet another *cerveza* and strippers bar with Tommy into something more Russ Swain friendly. I had picked up a rudimentary understanding of Spanish on my travels in Brazil, where Portuguese is the language, but Spanish connects, and while I was not going to win any Spanish oratorical contests, I could make myself understood. I needed to go out on the town and work the room, so to speak.

So, one night, at about 10 o'clock, I told Tommy that I was getting a headache, and needed to head back to our hotel. That wasn't true. I really wanted to get out into the town and mingle with the people, and to pump some of my $20s into Mazatlán's economy. And get some clean money back.

I hailed a taxi and got in. In Mazatlán, the taxis are souped up golf carts call *neumonia*, which means "pneumonia" in English because they are open air vehicles, and it's a dark little joke on what you can get from riding in them on one of Mazatlán's cold snowy nights (which never happen, hence the joke). Behind the wheel of the *neumonia* was a young guy, just 23 years old, named Marco. He looked different from a lot of people I saw, as he did not have that strong Hispanic-Indigenous mix of features so common in Mexico. He looked like a guy I might have seen in Ogden. He reminded me a bit of me.

So, more than wanting to launder money with him, I wanted to know a bit about him. As we were driving along the ocean, I asked Marco to tell me about himself and his life here. He told me he had grown up in Mazatlán and he had married his high school sweetheart. I thought about my own wife and daughters, and I asked him if they had children, and he told me that they were about to. As in, his wife was due that very night.

I immediately blurted "What the hell are you doing driving a cab?!!" I was astonished that he would be at work on such an important night. He said that it was fine, and that his wife's parents were at the hospital with her, but this only made me more agitated. I suddenly became a firebrand preacher, in my pulpit in the back of this golf cart taxi and told Marco in very plain Spanish that he had to rethink his life priorities at this very moment. I could always get another taxi, but he had to get to the hospital because he was not going to get another night when his first child was born.

He was surprised by my insistence, but he was also apologetic. He told me that with one more mouth to feed on the way, he couldn't afford to take the night off. It was his Catch-22. I asked him how much he made driving the cab each night and he said $30. So, I peeled off $30 and told him he was done for the night.

He shook his curly head and told me, no he wasn't. He had to make $200 in a night's work in order to get his cut of $30. So, I again produced my roll of Russ Swain $20s, and gave him another $200. And then I told him that since I had paid for his night, I was now in command of the cab. And since that was the case, we were now going where I wanted to go, and that was to the hospital where his wife was waiting to give birth.

So, we drove to the hospital. When we arrived, I congratulated Marco for listening to me, and said that I would catch another cab and make my way into the Mazatlán night while he was with his wife welcoming their child into the world. He told me that I had talked a lot of sense into him and thanked me for it. Then, he insisted that I come upstairs so he could introduce me to the imminent mother of his child.

I was curious to see what her reaction would be like when her husband walked through her door, so up the stairs we went to the floor on which Marco's wife was waiting to give birth. We walked down the hallway, and her door was open.

I was hard on Marco's heels as he entered her room, and I saw tears immediately well up in her big brown eyes. She had dark hair, and her lovely soft, gentle Hispanic face broke into an angelic kind of smile as she told him that she just knew he would come to be with her on this night. She was so happy.

Her parents were also there, and they gave Marco a different kind of look that said, "It's a good thing you showed up, you bastard, or the kid would be minus a father if you had not."

Marco turned to me and silently mouthed the word "gracias" and then introduced me to his wife, Maria, and her parents, Pablo and Inez. And then he took a page from the Book of Swain and told them a very creative story about how he came to be standing in front of them.

I was his American friend who knew the owner of the taxicab company, and in fact, had invested in it. So, I had influence with his boss, and, as the Sinaloa Cartel (Mazatlán is in Sinaloa) would not be established until 1986, my influence was not born of anything other than goodwill, and a little cash. Marco added that I was the father of many children back in the U.S., and so I had helped him to get off work because tonight I knew to the very depths of my soul why Marco being here, now, in the hospital for the birth of his first child, was so important. He then added his deep gratitude to me for knowing that he wanted to be responsible to his family, and how I had made that possible.

Maria and her parents thanked me, and I hung around speaking my basic Spanish with them about the joys of parenthood, and then said I would push off into the Mazatlán evening. I shook hands with Maria's parents, and patted his wife on the back, and wished them all a blessed night.

Marco said he would walk me to the door, and they all agreed that he could disappear for a bit as the baby was not yet trying to bust out. As we walked along the hallways, Marco thanked me again for making him realize where he was really supposed to be tonight, and then he totally surprised me.

My Hispanic friends could not properly say my name, Russ, as the "ss" sounded liked "th." So, they turned "Russ" into "Rocks" because it was easier for them to say. Marco said *"Ahorita,"* which means "right this moment" was so "important to me that when my *barone* arrives, I am going to nickname him 'Little Rocks' in honor of you. *Gracias, hermano.*" Thank you, friend.

So, when I am having a moment of solitude, reflecting on my life, I like to think that there is a Little Rocks somewhere in Mexico today, named after my small gesture of helping a man get to the birth of his child.

When I got back to the hotel, Tommy had returned from his night on the town, and he was happy to hear that my headache had retreated enough to let me go out myself.

So, I told him what I had done, with Marco the cabbie and his pregnant wife and our visit to the hospital. Tommy looked thoughtful as he listened to my story, and when I had finished, he said that I had done a good thing. Then he told me that he had a hospital visit in his future as well. His "health issue" was more than multiple sclerosis. He had been diagnosed with pancreatic cancer, which, then as now, kills fast. This trip to Mazatlán was going to be his last.

The news hit me hard, and I realized then how much of a friend Tommy considered me to be to invite me along on his adios tour of Mazatlán. I also realized that I considered Tommy the Shark to be my friend as well. But I had no idea how I could help him.

We had to come back to Utah a bit early because of Tommy's health, and I thought about how fragile life was on our flight back home. Little Rock was coming into the world on the same night that I learned Tommy would soon be leaving it. As the saying went, you just never knew, so you had to live every day as if it would be your last. Ironically, I had just started to live, thanks to my counterfeiting success, and I didn't want any day soon to be my last. But I got the point.

Tommy pretty much went straight into the hospital once we got home. They operated on him, but with pancreatic cancer, surgery is not effective if the cancer has metastasized to your lymph nodes or other organs. As it had with Tommy. The jig would soon be up.

On the home front, life was normal. My wife and daughters were happy, I sang the hymns in church, and business was solid at Para Graphics. I also had a lot of boxes stuffed with Russ Swain $20s, and I looked at them with affection, the way you might look at an old friend who was always reliable when you needed them. Did I have any urges to print some more money? No. Rather, not yet. That day would come, and it would, of course, come with consequences.

So, too, did my day with Tommy. I was at work when Tommy called me from the hospital. He always called me Swain, and he got straight to the point. "Swain, you always said you were my friend," he said, "and that you would do anything for me."

I agreed that I had said that. Another surprising development in my friendship with Tommy the Shark.

"Did you really mean it?" he asked me.

I told him that yes, of course I meant it. He then told me he was in the hospital at the state clinic, and that they would not let him leave. "I need you to come down and break me out," he said.

"When do you want me to come?"

And he said, "Right now.

I felt that old rush of adrenaline surge through my body. I was not going to test my $20s in a fresh market. I was going to break my friend Tommy the Shark out of jail. So, I got into my car and made the forty-minute drive down to the hospital in Salt Lake, taking care to keep to the speed limit. I did not want my jailbreak to be delayed by the law.

I arrived at the hospital and made my way up to Tommy's room. I had a black raincoat over my arm that I had brought along to cover his escape, but to anyone who noticed me, it just looked like I was carrying my own coat. I was wearing a sports jacket, so the raincoat just looked like me being prepared should the skies open up.

Tommy was lying in bed, looking miserable. He had a series of tubes hooked into his arm, delivering chemo, I guessed.

"Swain!" he exclaimed on seeing me, a smile breaking out on his face. It was a smile that showed his pleasure that I had done what I had promised.

"Let's get you out of here, Tommy," I said, looking around to make sure no nurse was about to walk in the door before I got Tommy out of bed and into the black raincoat.

"I guess we have to leave the tubes in until all that stuff has dripped into me."

I agreed. I didn't want to mess with what his doctors were doing. I just wanted to get him out of the hospital, and we could take his medicine, but not his clothes, as that would be too obvious.

We held the bags of drugs dripping into his veins as we walked down the hall to the elevator. Suddenly, this nurse stepped out of the shadows and right into our path. She was middle-aged and glowering, like Nurse Ratched who tormented Jack Nicholson's character in *One Flew Over the Cuckoo's Nest*.

"Where do you think you're going?" she asked, more with the tone of a suspicious beat cop than an oncology ward nurse.

I summoned up my best fair-haired Mormon boy smile and said, "My friend here is getting restless from lying around all day, so I'm just taking him for a walk. We are going to get a little circulation rolling for him, and he'll be better for it."

I did not want to convey that he was not getting anything but the best treatment here, so I held my smile as she looked at me and Tommy for a long beat. Then she smiled back. "You're a good friend. Enjoy your walk."

"Thank you," I said, offering a courtly bow of my head. "We will do that very thing."

Then I took Tommy's arm and walked him toward the elevators. As soon as we got there, one pinged its arrival, which was perfect timing, just like in the movies. And as the doors opened, we saw a couple more nurses and lab technicians already on board, taking in this tubed up patient in a black raincoat and his fair-haired grinning friend, just like in the movies.

The nurses and lab technicians made room for us, and we got in. One of the nurses noticed Tommy's hospital slippers and said, "Hope you don't plan on going for a hike!"

I grinned and fired back my new reason for our wander, one which had just popped into my head, as reasons seemed to do ever since I started my money business. "No danger of that," I said with a smile. "We're just going out for a smoke."

I was always amazed by the number of people you'd see smoking outside of hospitals, and thought we might tap into that, even if Tommy didn't smoke and neither did I.

It worked, as you could see their looks of pity now, conveying that Tommy had both a serious illness which they could gauge from the tubes of chemicals running into his arms, and a considerate buddy who was trying to speed up his decline with nicotine.

The rest of our descent was silent, and as we stepped out of the elevator, Tommy said with gusto, "I'd walk a mile for a Camel."

I had to bite back laughter, as he was referring to a famous line from the Camel cigarette ads, where a guy walks a mile through hostile terrain just to inhale the fumes of a Camel cigarette. I turned to him and gave him a wink, and once we were outside, I said, "You're not walking a mile."

So, with me holding Tommy's IV bags, the only walk we made was as fast as he could go to my car, and I eased him into the passenger seat. Then I got in behind the wheel and hit the gas and we were on our way. I had liberated Tommy the Shark from cancer captivity.

Without realizing it, Tommy had become my hero—taking life on his terms, not those dictated to him by this disease ravaging him. He was refusing to let cancer, or the doctors and nurses who had authority over him now to have authority over where he would die. He wanted to go out, at home, as his own man. Over time, we had slowly become connected by the bonds of a deep mutual history.

Once we cleared the parking lot, Tommy smiled like we were a couple of seasoned criminals on the lam.

Then he poked me in the arm and said, "I want beer."

I gave him a look. Beer? Really? In your condition?

He shrugged and explained. "I need to feel as if I have control of my life."

I gathered he wanted the portable kind, and not the pint he'd get when he was controlling loans action at the stripper bar, so I pulled up to a convenience store and asked him what kind of beer he wanted.

"Mexican, of course," he said with a smile. "Corona would be great."

I picked up a six-pack of Corona and got back in the car. "Where do you want to go now?" I asked.

Tommy picked up one of the beers, pretended it was open and raised it in my direction. "Thanks, Swain. Just take me home. If I'm going to die, that's where I want to be and not in some godforsaken hospital surrounded by strangers."

So, I drove Tommy home. He lived in a big, opulent house in the East Bench section of the city, at the base of the Wasatch Mountain range. It was a house befitting his status as a successful Shark. And it was my first time seeing it.

He had this big driveway which curled to reveal a lavish

abode. We entered a marble foyer, which led to a living room that was painted in a soft pink pastel, filled with stylish but comfortable furniture, with some fine landscape paintings on the wall. Tommy the Shark, for all his time doing his usurious business in the Happy Trails strip bar, had good taste. I realized upon seeing his home that Tommy, like me, had a double life.

We had been gone from the hospital for about forty-five minutes, so he had been absent for much longer than a smoke break or a short circulation reviving walk. The hospital had figured out that Tommy had bolted, and after looking everywhere for him, had called his wife, Launi. She did not know where Tommy was as he had not let her in on his escape plan. She was frantic when we arrived, and then, she was furious.

Launi was an attractive woman a couple of years younger than Tommy, so closer in age to me. She was slim and blonde, and her pretty face was contorted in anger at what this man had put her through, and now she just let him have it. How could he be so thoughtless? How could he put her through this?

Tommy let her have it back. How could she not see how he was suffering? I just let them unload on each other for a while, until there was a pause, and I could step in as the referee. Tommy was coming to the end of his days, and I didn't want them to be filled with this domestic tension, so I took it upon myself to become a kind of marriage counselor to my Shark and his wife.

"I just need to say something at this point," I began, and they both looked at me in surprise, as if they had forgotten that I was even there. "Tommy," I continued, "you need to realize that this is not all about you, and Launi, you need to realize this isn't all about you, either. It's about all of us and how Tommy's illness is affecting us all."

I had their attention, so I continued. "Tommy, you need to see that Launi is facing the realization that she could soon be losing her mate. She will be on her own, taking care of your children and herself once you have left them, and you need to see how worrisome that is for her."

Tommy looked at me as if I had just said the unsayable, but he wasn't angry. He gave me a curt nod and a smile. So, I went on. "And Launi, you need to understand that Tommy feels bad, not just physically bad, but emotionally bad that this is happening to him, and to you, and he's tried his best to stop it, but right now, the disease has the higher number on the scoreboard."

Launi looked at me as if I had opened a door for her, so since I now had a receptive audience, I went deeper. The Shark owed his wife love. "Launi, you also need to know how much Tommy loves you. I know he doesn't share that with you often, but I know how much he loves you because he has told me."

Launi, with tears in her eyes, looked at her husband and said, "Really, Tommy?"

Tommy, with tears in his eyes, replied "Well, I told you six years ago that I loved you. Nothing has changed."

I needed to step in fast after that alarming qualification, and so I said "Tommy, you tell me how much you love and adore your wife all the time. Why don't you tell her now?"

So, he did. He told her that she was the only woman he had truly ever loved. Launi seemed to have grown younger by a decade at hearing this, and now they were sitting on the couch and hugging and crying, and Russ Swain, Counterfeiter and Marriage Counselor, realized it was time for me to leave. And maybe to bring some of my own marital wisdom to bear on my own house.

But that afternoon in Salt Lake City, I had seen reality change. I got Tommy where he wanted to be, at home, and I got him and his wife to really talk to each other about their feelings. I had created a new reality, which was just like I had done with my counterfeit $20s. If you believed it was real, then you would make it so.

Sadly, I could not change Tommy's physical reality beyond changing his GPS. He died about three weeks after I brought him home. And home is where he wanted to be when the time came, and I took solace in that fact. But I was grieving the loss of a man who had transformed himself from my frightener to my friend.

Launi, however, was not finished with me. She had one more surprise in store. She asked me to say the prayer at Tommy's funeral. I said yes. I would do that.

The church, in the East Bench, was pretty full for Tommy's funeral, not because Tommy had a lot of people in mourning for him. It was because Mormons support each other in life and death and so the congregation of his wife's church came out for her husband Tommy, who was not religious, but since she was a member of their community, she needed their support. Tommy's friend Rhino was not at the funeral, as he had cheated Tommy on a real estate deal and so was no longer a friend. Which meant that as I scanned the crowd, I realized that I was his only friend who was there. And that maybe, I was his only friend.

The bishop read from the Book of Mormon, and I gave the prayer, which is really a eulogy. I told everyone that Tommy was a good guy, though I did not get into how he met and how that changed my reality, and that in the end, he was a decent man who wanted to do well for his family. I told everyone how much he loved his wife and children, who were there in the front row, a son and daughter leaning against their mother in their sadness, but also in their Mormon hope that one day they would see Tommy again in the afterlife. Of course, my own family was not there, because I could not reveal to them that I knew Tommy in life, and now in death.

His wife Launi never remarried. About once a year, she messages me on Facebook Messenger. And it's always about Tommy, talking about him as if they had the love affair of the century. And that's her reality, the one she has carried forward. The reality that I helped to cement.

As I drove back to my own family from Tommy's funeral, I thought about how much I loved them, and how I hoped we would be together for a long time. I was feeling good about my life, and our prospects, and knew that so long as I played it carefully, nothing could get in the way of my family's happiness. Of course, I was wrong about that, and I was wrong for one of the best reasons. I was about to experience a profound change of my own reality, and in a most unexpected way.

6

Warren and John

My own journey to where I am today took a turn in the road, quite literally, when I acquired Warren, which was the name I gave to an old Chevy pick-up truck I had bought for $300 Russ Swains from a neighbor who was moving to California. I called it Warren after Warren Beatty, an actor whom I admired, and with a sense of irony, as Beatty was movie star handsome, and this truck was quite the opposite. It was a battered old blue thing that looked like it had lost many battles. I figured it would conk out on me before the seasons changed, but I felt something move me to say yes to my friend and so Warren and I became mates.

I was, as I have been once or twice before, wrong about how long Warren would roll with me, and wrong about what he would do to my own reality. I was living in our nice little cottage style house in Ogden's East Bench neighborhood with its white picket fence and koi filled pool my wife had designed and built, and the Wasatch mountains rising up in majesty around us. life was good. The neighbors were friendly, my daughters had pals they connected with and things between me and my wife were good. Or maybe not as good as they had been, as she said I seemed distant at times.

Of course, I was distant, as I was in two places at once. I was living two lives, still laundering my Russ Swain $20s—and I had a lot of them left —while also running my graphic design business like the most solid citizen in the county.

I had other cars, of course, and Warren was my side hustle kind of vehicle as I did have a conventional car, but he was much more than that. Warren and I bonded, and he let me get even more distant, by roaming the Utah roads and thinking about what I wanted to do next. Of course, Warren had his own plans that would soon change mine, and then, change my life.

I had Warren in hand for about a week when a neighbor called and said he had seen my hearty blue pick-up truck parked out front of our house. He wanted to borrow it to haul some stuff to the dump. In those days, the 1980s, people felt more connected. We knew our neighbors. We wouldn't hesitate to ask them to bring in our mail and newspapers when we went away for a few days. We were in the habit of lending a hand when we saw someone in need. We trusted more. We knew who we could ask for help, and they knew we would reciprocate. So, when my neighbor asked to borrow Warren, I said "of course."

This neighborly act on my part unleashed a deluge upon me. I was taking so many calls from neighbors who wanted to borrow Warren—some of whom I couldn't even pull out of a police lineup—that I had to create a schedule for my old blue pick-up. "Morning or afternoon? Hold on, there's another call coming in. Let me put you on hold." I swear that Warren had an infrared beacon attached to his roof that broadcast messages that beamed out to all we passed by "Hello! My name is Warren, and I am here to serve you. Please don't hesitate to ask me for anything!"

As for me, I got to hang out with Warren during the week, when demand was less for his services. One midweek morning, I stopped at the Seven-Eleven to fuel up Warren. I went inside to pay for the gas, and I was approached by a derelict old woman. She had several teeth missing and looked like she was hanging onto the sides of the planet with suction cups.

"Excuse me sir," she said, "but is that your blue truck outside, at the pump?"

I answered with a courtesy she did not expect. Or maybe she did. "Well yes ma'am, it is," I said.

She smiled at me like I was her favorite child. "When I saw that truck, I knew that a kind soul owned it. I need a ride up to the local hospital to get some stitches taken out of my thumb. Would you be so kind as to give me a ride?"

She had clocked me as a kind soul because of whatever Warren was beaming out. I could say, "no, you're mistaken, I'm a ruthless counterfeiter," or I could accept her verdict. I chose the latter.

"Certainly," I said. "Let me get the door for you." I helped her up into Warren and then got in and turned on the engine and let him digest a bit of his fuel. I asked her, "What happened to your thumb?"

The woman looked down, and then smiled shyly at me. "I'm a bit embarrassed to say, but I found a pack of cigarettes. Suddenly, this woman came outta nowhere and tried to take 'em. She's a street person, like me. I would not let her take 'em." She nodded, pleased with her resolve. Then she added, "That's when she bit me."

I had started to drive away but then I hit the brakes. My passenger looked at me as if I was going to throw her out for her revelation of this predictable street person truth. Instead, I had something else in mind. "I am sorry, ma'am," I said, "but where are my manners? I'll bet you haven't had your morning coffee yet!"

She relaxed and leaned back into Warren's embrace. Then, she said simply, "Don't have money for no coffee."

I gave her a smile to reassure her that this was no obstacle to her getting some caffeine. "A gentleman should always pay for the lady's coffee. You watch the truck and I'll be right back. Do you take cream and sugar?"

She did take cream and sugar, and while I did not drink coffee, I was happy to deliver it. My passenger was so happy with her coffee that she grinned at me like I had restored her toothless faith in humanity. Suddenly, I had entered a new phase of my life with Warren.

It was almost as if I now had a special calling, in addition to counterfeiting—which I wasn't doing anymore, but I was still enjoying its fruits. Sure, I had gone into the darkness, but Warren was helping to bring me back into the light. Indeed, my new role in life is best expressed by this Warren-inspired mantra that I soon created: "As the owner of Warren, it's my sworn duty to offer whatever assistance is needed to anybody who asks." And ask, they did.

Warren didn't have air conditioning, so in the summer months, I drove him around town with the windows down. On one occasion, I was driving downtown, slowing to stop for a red light. A guy on the sidewalk called out, "Hey you! You in the truck, pull OVER!"

I turned my head and saw a guy in his mid-20s, lean and fit, who didn't look homeless. He was wearing Levi's and a T-shirt, and he had a tool belt and a little bag of tools. He looked like he was going to a building site.

"Me?" I said, pointing to myself?

"Yeah! Pull your truck over!"

I assumed that there was something wrong, like maybe I had a flat tire, or I was dragging something, and so I did as he instructed. I pulled the truck next to the curb and then the guy who pulled me over started loading his tools in the back of Warren. Then he opened the passenger door and climbed into the cab. "Boy, it's hot out there!" he said.

I was astonished. "Excuse me, but do I know you?!?" I asked.

"Oh, sorry, my name is Jack. I saw this truck and I thought, that guy drivin' it will give me a ride! I wasn't wrong, was I?"

The mantra of Warren kicked in. "Nah, Jack, you weren't wrong." I put the truck in gear. "Where to?"

Jack needed a ride to the Marion Hotel, not far from the train station. The Marion was a century old, and in its heyday, had been a playground for the hookers, the hoodlums and the hucksters from the Al Capone era. It was on 25th Street, which had been Ogden's pathway to vice, and once upon a time was known as "Two Bit Street" across the United States due to its reputation for gambling and prostitution along Electric Alley.

It actually kicked into life after the railway station opened in 1889 at the end of 25th Street. People on the many trains which stopped in Ogden, then a railway hub, would get out to stretch their legs and wander up the street to see what they could see. As a result of this traffic, restaurants, shops, rooming houses and the Marion Hotel all opened up to serve their needs, along with the palaces of vice.

By the time I was driving Jack to the Marion, the hotel had become a run-down refuge for down-on-their-luck wanderers and junkies.

As I pulled into the parking lot, Jack thanked me and hopped out of Warren. Friends, who did not look like fellow workers, but maybe fellow travelers of a sort, all of them barely scraping by, came over to help him unload his tools. Assuming that I was just another one of their tribe, they greeted me. "Yo, Duuuude! That's a nice truck you got there!"

Not wanting to come across to these guys as someone of more privilege, even if I did have a quarter of a million dollars of fake money stashed in business card boxes in my shop, I downplayed myself and Warren. "Oh, it's not much, really—in fact, I only paid three-hundred bucks for it."

That wasn't exactly the downplay I had intended, as the man exclaimed "Dude! Where'd you get three hundred bucks!!?"

I was new at counterfeiting and I wasn't reckless with it,

so I did not hand over some Russ Swain $20s. I had promised myself that I would never spend any of those bills in Ogden, nor was I trying to be a modern-day Robin Hood. But I was flush enough that I could show a little generosity by saying, "Here's a few bucks, Jack, (a ten, a five and a couple of ones). Buy you and your friends a cold one on me. Who knows, I might need a favor someday."

They were grateful, and immediately reciprocated by asking me to hang around and enjoy some of the weed that a friend of theirs would soon be lighting up for them all. I had to decline as weed was not in my repertoire, so to speak, but I had realized that by bringing Jack to the Marion, and getting invited to hang with them, I had been admitted, just a little bit, to their tribe. Thanks to Warren.

And then, almost as if by magic, Warren raised the bar on it all.

Some well-heeled friends of mine had purchased a cabin in a wooded area called Island Park, just outside of West Yellowstone on Henry's Fork of the Snake River. It offers lots of incredible fishing and hunting and outdoor activities.

An interior designer had referred me to them to do some work on their house, and we just clicked. They were a wealthy married couple with no kids and two dogs, and they bought this small cabin from a young guy as a place for them to go fishing, but then one thing led to another, and they started to remodel it.

They dumped a couple of hundred thousand dollars into landscaping and decorating and made it look like Ralph Lauren owned it. They had asked me to come up to paint a mural of a moose on the wall, because they had begun to use the cabin for social gatherings and wanted to give the place some rustic character. So, I loaded Warren up with paints, brushes, and sprayers, and we hit the road early to get a running start.

Dawn was breaking under gray skies with a light rain falling, but even so, I enjoyed being awake at the birth of a new day. As I pulled onto the freeway entrance, there was a man, in his late twenties, sitting atop his bedroll that was neatly rolled-up, brandishing a cardboard sign that read "Yellowstone."

In those days, hitchhiking was a viable option, as a way of getting around. From the time I learned to drive, I have picked up hitchhikers. And many were the times that I relied on passersby to help me arrive at my destinations, as well. As they say nowadays, 'it's just how we rolled.'

It's how Warren rolled, too. He pretty much pulled himself over to give the young man a ride. The Yellowstone bound traveler was gregarious, cheerful, and he expressed gratitude for my having stopped. He was instantly likable, and I knew I was going to enjoy his company for the next few hours.

As we became acquainted. I learned that his name was Kevin, and he had traveled all over America counting on the luck of a good right thumb. When he was in his teens, he had worked in a vineyard that his family owned. He had learned to speak fluent Spanish, as he picked grapes alongside the migrant workers. But then his father died unexpectedly. And Kevin's uncle, who owned the remaining interest, sold the vineyard.

The young man never cared much for the uncle so he "lit-out-for-the-territories." He had no idea where he was going. He pointed his toes and told his heels to follow, trusting that the universe would help him find his destiny. He wasn't a hobo, nor was he a beggar. He found work wherever he went. When I asked him what he did to pass the time while he was waiting for a ride, he said, "I read. I'm a voracious reader."

"Yeah? Who's your favorite author?" I inquired. "Anybody I would know?"

He grinned with such pleasure that it was as if I—or Warren—had just asked the one question he most wanted to answer. "My favorite author," Kevin began, "is a guy that I believe to be the principal voice of the American counterculture, especially when it comes to delivering the ideas that thrived during the drug-induced sixties. I rarely encounter anyone who's read him, but I love him. His name is Tom Robbins."

Now it was my turn to grin. I am not an omnivorous reader but I like what I like and I had always loved Tom Robbins since ANOTHER ROADSIDE ATTRACTION. "Tom Robbins is MY favorite author! Which books have you read?"

"All of 'em."

"Me too! Which was your favorite? Wait, wait... don't answer, let me guess... JITTERBUG PERFUME!"

"Actually, yeah. That's right, followed by... STILL LIFE WITH..."

"WOODPECKER!" We both chimed in unison.

At that point I turned on my blinker, indicating I was getting off at the next exit.

Now his joy turned to apprehension as he saw we were exiting the freeway. "Ah... is my ride... over?

"Not at all," I laughed. "There's a Flying J Truckstop here in Snowville and it occurred to me that you haven't had breakfast. Let's get some food to start our journey off right."

"Great," he said, clearly relieved. "But just so you know, I've got money. Let's each cover our own," he said. I agreed.

Kevin ordered scrambled eggs, giving me a hint of what was to come by saying, "The best thing about scrambled eggs is, no matter how they land, they're always sunny side up." And from then on, we had one of the most stimulating, upbeat, animated conversations that I had ever had.

Our talk focused on the concept of the dynamic balance of opposites throughout the universe. How light and dark, hot and cold, and good and evil all needed to coexist as a kind of cosmic definition of themselves and the other. But that even with this universal governor, we were still under grave threat—from ourselves.

It was a threat I had spent much time considering. Had

what I had done become my biggest threat to myself? I did not know. But I wanted to hear more from Kevin, so I redirected the conversation a little.

"What are the most impressive changes in the country that you've seen?" I asked him, taking a sip of orange juice.

"Well," he said, coming back to his theme. "I'll tell you exactly what that is. People of my generation have traded the God of the Old Testament for the God of technology. We want instant gratification; we want to pray to technology for that thing that will give us a fix right now."

I thought about how I had used technology to get myself out of a fix. Where was the Old Testament God in my counterfeiting?

"The God of the Old Testament had to prepare His prophet or His messenger," Kevin continued, "by steeping them in wisdom through a gradual process of enlightenment. The God of technology doesn't believe in such nonsense." And, he continued, it will be the God of technology who destroys us all. "Because eventually, some guy is going to create a smart bomb in his garage that will be capable of blowing us all up. Or we'll invent some super robot and ask it to create world peace and the robot brain will go, 'Aha, that's easy. Kill all the humans.' "

I felt that I was seated before some kind of New Age guru.

Kevin was one of the most charismatic people I had ever met. He seemed to cast a net of enchantment over everything in life. Even the waitress was swooning over him. "Seems that our waitress is quite taken with you, my friend."

"I am not sorry that, on some occasions, women desire my company. Nor am I sorry that I enjoy the company of the loveliest of them. It's all part of the story I am telling as I go."

Thanks to Warren, I had encountered a person who was showing me how to look at life with more poetic awareness and psychological depth than ever before. I was able to momentarily look past the neon signs and strip malls and see inside our world.

Outwardly, Kevin appeared to have so little. But that was not his perspective. As he put it, "I'm living my life out of my own imagination, creating it with purpose and intent, every day. In that sense, I'm playing God. I am my own Creator. I was surprised at how easy the act of leaving was, and how good it felt. Walking away gives you freedom. This world is rich with possibilities, and as I explore it, I'm not encumbered with stuff. We build these permanent dwellings that need to be filled with possessions. We become trapped by them. We lose our mobility and our ability to live freely in the world."

His view was very different from the one I had known growing up, where one's faith meant that you worked to serve family and community before you thought about yourself. I had done that, and I had not. I liked it, but I was also profoundly moved by Kevin's gift. He had turned what would've been a mundane road trip into a journey of deeper awareness.

I dropped him off at Yellowstone and thanked him for his company. "You have made this trip into one I shall never forget," I told him.

He smiled at me and said "You had a hand in it, too, Russ. If you hadn't stopped on the road to give me a lift, this story would not have been told."

And then, with a wave and a smile, he trudged off to the next chapter of his story. I could see, I thought, a swirl of diamond dust around him, one that the wind had lifted and then blew gently over Warren's hood and up onto the windshield, so that I was looking through its magic as I considered what I had learned.

I was beginning to understand how we're all tribal—and that beater pickup truck was a symbol that gave recognition that I was just another one of a large band of gypsies, making my way, living on the edge, getting by on my wits. I could be approached and maybe counted on to help if I could. It's not unlike the tribe we call church or political party or those who love the 49ers. We need to belong. And we need to connect.

I thought about what Kevin had said about himself. He was his own Creator. I, too, in many ways, had become my own Creator, too. Would I now destroy what I had created?

That question meant that I now had to ask myself: "What would I really like to do with my life? How could I take the talent with which I had been blessed, and do something good?" Or was I already doing good, even though I had done something that the world thought was bad? My view of myself was fuzzy, and I needed clarity. Once again, Warren came to the rescue.

I had long finished the moose mural in Island Park, and I was now back home in Ogden. It was winter, and snow was falling as I drove Warren to a client's house to pick up a check. As I was rolling along, I noticed this Black kid, wearing just a light jacket, walking along, hunched against the cold. He looked miserable. I wondered why no one was stopping to offer that guy a ride?

I picked up the check, and had a quick chat with the client, and on my way back, saw the same kid still walking, looking even more miserable as the wet snow came swirling down upon him.

I just pulled right up alongside the kid, reached over to the door handle, then swung open the passenger door. I yelled at him through the now howling snow to get in. He didn't hesitate.

I turned up the heat to warm him up, and I said, "You must not be from around here. You're not dressed for this kind of weather."

"No, I'm from Oregon," he replied, shivering.

"What are you doing here?" I asked.

He was a tall Black youth with an easy smile who said he had come to Weber State on a track scholarship. I was impressed, but he deflected that. "If you knew anything about the neighborhood that I grew up in, then the first thing you'd know that I learned how to do is to run real fast."

I thought that was funny, in a dark way, and I liked him. His name was James. I asked him where I could drive him, and he said to the bus station. I asked if he was going back to Oregon and he said no, he was staying put. He had an apartment and had been out looking for work when the snow started to fall.

"But it's interesting," he said, "for as I was walking along, I had a thought. I asked God, 'If y'all knows when a sparrow falls out of a tree, did y'all know that it's snowing on me?' A minute after I think this, you pulled up and offered me a ride."

It was an interesting observation. He had just connected me and Warren to God's plan.

We drove on, and he pointed out his church.

"Are you a religious man, Mr. Russ?" He called me Mr. Russ.

"Not so much," I replied. The last thing I wanted was for James to proselytize to me as we drove in the snow. After Kevin's vision of the world, I didn't need a roof and altar to believe.

"That's too bad," he said. "The reason I asked is that I'm the organist for my church, and people tell me that I'm a good organist. I don't know a lot of people outside of the church. But it'd be nice if you would come and hear me play sometimes."

That struck a chord with me. It would be an interesting experience to show up at his Black Baptist Church and listen to this young man play the organ. So, when Sunday came, I threw on a necktie and a sports jacket, and told my wife I was going to meet a client. She gave me a funny look, as I never dressed up in a jacket and tie to see a client, but I told her it was a "big job." She accepted that and said she would take the girls to church. So, I got into Warren and headed over to New Zion Baptist Church on Lincoln Avenue to hear James play the organ.

People smiled and nodded in welcome to me when I walked in. The church had a different vibe than the Mormon churches I had been in. First of all, I was the only white person in the place. Secondly, there was music serenading the congregation from the moment I entered. And thirdly, I knew the guy sitting at the organ.

My goodness, James could play the organ as if it was part of his very being, making the notes roll and soar and smash and tiptoe all with the magic in his hands. It was electrifying.

So, too, was the sermon. The pastor, a middle-aged Black man, spoke with a passion and a captivating eloquence that had the congregation murmuring—or even shouting out—Amen! as he offered his thoughts on how we all connected to God. I realized that I could listen to this pastor for as long as he wanted to preach, such were his gifts at oratory. And at holiness. He believed in what he was telling us: God loved us all, even if we didn't do such a good job of loving each other.

As the pastor preached, James played these rolling chords beneath his words. Then, James raised his hand. He had something to say. So, the pastor, again showing that the congregation was more important than what he had to say, invited him to the pulpit. So, James rose from the organ, and walked to the pulpit and spoke to the congregation.

"Brothers and sisters," he began, and smiled at me. "I want to say I invited a new brother to be with us today. And he's a white brother, you know?"

All of a sudden, everybody was looking over at where James was looking, and I felt a little bit self-conscious, so I gave a small wave to indicate, in case anyone had not figured it out, that I was that white guy.

And then, in no more than two minutes, James gave a speech that I can hear in my heart still.

"I want to talk about God's power and how sometimes he

likes to hide it, you know, in the decisions that we make. For instance, last week, that white brother that's sitting among you today, he made a decision to stop his car and offer a ride to a Black man that he didn't even know, because it was snowing real hard."

"To him, that might have seemed like no big deal. Like it was just a small decision, but you have no idea of knowing how huge that small decision affected me. You know, a boy who was so far away from home that I didn't even feel like God knew where I was anymore. But He knew. And the white brother was God in action."

"I think God's gonna put all of us in that same situation, where we have to make a decision to be kind to somebody. And, you know, I want to thank the white brother for being kind to me, because I think God sometimes hides some of his greatest power in those things that seem so small."

James's words powerfully affected me. I thanked James on the way out of church and he shook my hand—everyone shook my hand. I didn't feel embarrassed; I felt like I was given a gift. By becoming a counterfeiter, I was free from who I was and could find out who I might be. I had made my own passport to all worlds. I had been driven more by restlessness and curiosity than altruism, but the multi-cultural uniqueness—strangeness even, that I discovered while on the road with Warren, by seeing these little pocket universes that make up my society, fascinated me. Perhaps these people that I met along the way were the heroes, in the way that they powerfully affected me. What more could I do to reciprocate?

John the Printer gave me my chance, and in my reciprocation, I changed my own world once again.

When I had decided to make my own $20 bills, I knew that I had to keep it all to myself if I wanted to stay out of prison. Just one person besides me knowing what I had done was dangerous enough, and I had already broken that rule with Tommy the Shark. And Tommy the Shark was dead and had taken my secret to his grave.

But my friend John the Printer, who had sold me the press upon which I minted the currency of Swain, was in trouble. Bigger trouble than when he had last asked me to buy him out. He was so distraught about running his new business that he had run it into the ground. While he was a genius printer, he was not so interested in applying that genius to business. He had about $30,000 worth of debt, owing money to suppliers, and if he didn't pay them, he was going to lose his house, which would put him and his wife Carrie and their two kids in very bad straits.

I had not helped him the first time he had asked me. I had filed it away and forgotten it. But now the shame of that action colored my cheeks, for John had asked me for help again. If I had taken action the first time, would he be in such dire straits now? I did not know. All I knew was that I could help him now. And that I would.

After all, not only had John sold me the printing equipment that changed my life, but he also introduced me to the woman who would become my wife.

Of course, she knew nothing about what I had done to buy her all those tampons, and she would never know because she would be destroyed if she knew. Not only that, I also didn't want to put her in any kind of legal danger, should the law ever come for me.

John, on the other hand, was no threat because he was so desperate. I called him up and lowballed the solution to his problems. In fact, I made his problem disappear into one of my own. "John, I'm in a really bad bind here," I said, my voice tense. "You're the only guy I know who can help me out. And if you will help me to fix my problem, you can enjoy the fruits of my fix. Come on over to my shop, and I will explain."

John came over to my shop after hours. He was the most average looking guy in all of Utah. Nobody would pick him out of a police lineup as the suspect, even if he had done the crime. Medium height, build, brown hair, brown eyes, and no distinguishing marks or scars. He was very forgettable. His wife, Carrie, was forgettable too. Very ordinary. To me, John was a sorry but talented man who had fallen on hard times and who had a family to support. He needed my help.

When he came to my shop, I spelled it out to him: we were going to make fake money. He didn't like the idea and left. I had not told him that I had already made fake money, so I didn't feel that he was going to go to the police, because he had what? He had heard about a counterfeiting plan? That would not fly, but I hoped that John would see the same kind of reason that I had seen in a solution that had saved me.

The next day, John came back to me and said, "You know what? I've slept on it. I think I need to do everything that's in my power to solve some problems as well."

I knew he had talked to his wife Carrie about it, and she had probably gone berserk at his refusal to accept what I offered. She was the one who told him to get back to my shop and to get on with it.

What I did with John was to pretend that I had never done this counterfeiting adventure before. I didn't have business card boxes stuffed with my Russ Swain $20s. I had just begun, and I had some ideas, but I needed his help.

I said, "John, this is how far I have taken it so far. I have the right paper, I have the color, I have the fibers printed on the paper, I have everything."

He studied what I had in hand, nodding in approval.

And I have jumped through hoops trying to get these really infinitely small white dots and black dots to make it look like a gravure," I said, showing him a real bill with its dots, the kind I was trying to reproduce.

John said, "Well, let me see what I can do."

He adjusted the pressure of the rollers, as I knew he would, and when the bills came off the press, he was taken aback. "Whoa," he said. "This looks just like money."

And I said, "Watch this. I've got this magical powder.

Diamond dust. It's got a fine grip to it. And it doesn't gum the rollers when you mix it with the ink. And watch what happens."

So, we ran a batch of bills with the diamond dust ink on them and John was just knocked out by these $20s. I had just given him the key to the kingdom. It was a pleasure seeing the joy of possibility on John's face now that he had that key in hand.

However, he used the key to close the door. John didn't want to be partners with me in this counterfeiting enterprise or anything like that. He just wanted to take enough money to get himself back on his feet, so he took $40,000. I told him how to wash it, away from Ogden, and how to be careful when he was doing the laundry.

"There are only six serial numbers on the bills," I told him, "so you never want to wash seven of them in the same place, or you will get a duplicate, and if someone is watching, well, could be trouble." He said he understood. And that we would never speak of this again. I agreed.

I watched him go off into the night with his $40,000 in fake money, and I felt good. I felt that I had saved John and his family. The kindness that had come to me from Warren the truck now played out in the world on my terms, as had the wisdom I had gained from the people whom Warren had led me to. Once again, I saw how diamond dust had worked its magic.

Of course, on that balmy Spring night, I had no inkling that I had just unleashed the seeds of my own destruction. But I had done so, as I would soon find out. And as you can see from reading this story, the destruction wasn't complete. I'm still here. But my reality was about to get radically changed.

7

Diamond Dusted

I had gone to Idaho one weekend to disperse some of my Russ Swain $20 bills and had a great trip. I had done a good load of money washing, rinsing about $2,000 in the various shops in Sun Valley, and was particularly pleased with a new pair of sunglasses I had picked up that made me look rather dashing, I thought, the kind that a fighter pilot might wear, with their gold rims and serious curves, like a jet making a tight turn in combat. They were expensive, but I had washed $300 in buying them, so I was feeling good about myself and the world. I mean, I had solved my problem, and I had solved John's problem. I had even made Tommy the Shark into a friend and had comforted him in his final days.

My family was healthy and happy, and my wife had a nice new car that made good old Warren look even homelier in comparison, so I would never park him too close to hers so as not to embarrass my faithful truck. My wife and daughters knew nothing about my counterfeit money and my washing of it. Just that I had lots of clients in Idaho, which is a lovely place, but they were happy to let me go there solo. It just doesn't have the same sparkle for kids as if I had clients in, let's say Disneyland. Everyone was happy to let me drive off on weekends to be with my clients in the Gem State, enjoying the effects of my own gem, diamond dust.

So, when I got back to Ogden, I was on top of the world. Until I walked through the door to my white picket fence house and saw the look on my wife's face. She looked like someone had died, but no, she said, everyone was fine. Or as fine as they could be. And then she told me.

Her parents called my wife to tell her that my printer friend John had been arrested for passing counterfeit bills. In Las Vegas. I took in this news without revealing anything. But inside, I was furious. I had helped John and he had done this?

Not only had John been arrested, but the Secret Service were looking for me, and called my wife's parents to tell them why. They then discovered $50,000 of not completely burned $20 bills in their word burning stove. You will recall that I had mentioned earlier in this tale that I had misunderstood the mechanics of the wood burning stove. And now that misunderstanding had come home, as they say, to roost. My wife's parents had put those burned bills all together with the help of the Secret Service, who now wanted to talk to me. I was supposed to call them.

I felt that the wind had been knocked-out of me. My breath was knotted. I went so far as to drop to my knees. I was stunned and stung. I was sickened by a sense of fear and loss, and I was even angry that my secret was exposed and brought to an end. I saw my future all too clearly, inside a gray prison, wife and girls long gone, and alone with my regrets for the next twenty years.

The Secret Service knew that John was from Ogden, had sold printing equipment to me, and took it from there. They connected those dots. I knew that I was busted, because if they had John, then they also had me. I didn't know, and to this day, still do not know, if he gave me up. He had made that counterfeit money in my shop, with me. I had told him how to wash it, and told him how to be careful, and thought he would have the wit to do just that thing with the $40,000 that we had made to solve his problems. But no, he decided to go to Las Vegas with his wife Carrie and wash it there.

I had put a varnish on the bills to prevent the blacklight counterfeit bill readers that casinos in Nevada used from spotting my fakes, but John and Carrie had not gone to casinos. No, they had been going each weekend to a shopping mall, the same shopping mall, and going from shop to shop, handing over $20s, and getting clean money back. John had told me that he understood my washing instructions, but clearly, he had not understood a thing.

Of course, his behavior attracted the attention of mall security, who thought John and Carrie might be kiting checks. The security people checked them out and saw that they were not exchanging checks from bank accounts with insufficient funds for goods. So, they let them go.

But John and Carrie kept coming back, and security took another look at their $20 bills. And of course, they spotted the one flaw in my Russ Swain $20s. I had no serial numbering machine, so the six serial numbers that I used repeated themselves. All you had to do, to be extra careful, was not use two bills with the same serial number in any transaction. I had explicitly told John that. He had seen it with his own eyes. How could he have been so careless?

So, now the Secret Service wanted to speak to me, as my wife had just told me. Now I had to tell my wife the truth. You might wonder why I didn't just bolt to Mexico. I had enough cash. But I loved my family too much to do that to them. And now I had to tell my wife that out of love, I had done this to them.

She listened to me in silence as I told her how and why I had created my Russ Swain $20s. She must have known as I explained the diamond dust story that she had helped me to spread that money around, but she did not yell and scream at me for making her an accomplice. She just looked so very sad. And to her great and wonderful credit, she said that we would protect the girls from whatever was going to happen, and that we would get through it. Which we did, and then we didn't.

My father had died by this point in my life, and his passing had happened when I worked at the advertising agency. He was 76 years old, and in poor health from his years of alcohol abuse, but my mother was very much alive. My devout Mormon mother, who raised me to be a good and faithful member of the church, and who had done everything she could do for me. And she would never see, nor could she have imagined, what was coming from me.

However, since I did not want her to hear about what I had done from anyone other than me, so I went to her house, the house in which I had grown up. I was still her little angel, and now I was going to have to confess that I was no longer that. Not even close.

I walked up to the single-story red brick rambler house, with its low-pitched roof, and its extended eaves and large windows. This was a classic Middle America home that had sprung up across the country after World War II and I remembered being happy here. Now I was going to walk into this Middle American home and tell my mother that her Angel Boy was in fact not that at all and make her very unhappy.

Melba was at first delighted to see me, a smile illuminating her kind and gentle face at first, and then I asked if we might sit down. She could see from the sadness on my face and heaviness in my voice that I had something serious to tell her, and so, her face grew grave. "I've got some really horrible news that's going to be very disappointing to you," I said.

"Don't be silly, you know you can't disappoint me," she said, giving me that smile I knew so well, one from earliest childhood told me I could do no wrong. I don't know what she imagined I was going to say, maybe that I had lost my business, or that my wife had left me, or that I had left her.

All I truly knew was that she would never have imagined the "something very wrong" I had done and was now about to reveal. And I couldn't even think about whether she would ever forgive me.

As I revealed the truth of my situation, I watched her lovely face furrow in sorrow. She suddenly looked a decade older, no longer pushing eighty, but suddenly into her nineties, as if my news had sped her closer to the end of her life. But then her face shifted again, and she took a deep breath. Then she showed the resolve I had seen her show around this very house when things were tough with my father, and she gave me a motherly smile, one of both admonition, and love.

"I'll love you unconditionally, no matter what," Melba Swain said to her baby. "But I am truly disappointed that you saw counterfeiting money as your only option."

My mother was a retired schoolteacher whose husband had, in his way, taken more than he left her with. And now, she realized her angel son had given her gifts she had just learned must have been bought with bad money. Even so, when I had my crisis that led to counterfeiting there was no way I could have gone to her to ask her to bail me out of my brochure fiasco. I had come up with a solution based on the talents I had inherited from her, though I had turned my inherited talent, as they say, into something all my own. I was grateful for her generous response, but in very short order I had let down the two women who were most important to me in the world. There was only one thing left for me to do: go forward and prepare myself for prison.

The Secret Service agent who ran my case was a guy in his forties named Roger Rodak. He was from Salt Lake City, and he was also a Mormon, though he had no interest in using our religion against me. Roger just wanted to know the truth.

Roger Rodak was no swaggering enforcer of justice, though, who tried to intimidate me with bluster and threats.

He was more like Agent Smith in *The Matrix*, not that he was a computer virus, but he was a black suit, white shirt, and dark tie guy. He looked and acted more like an accountant than a Secret Service agent who was investigating international counterfeiting rings like mine.

That's what Roger and his team thought they were dealing with at first, an international group of criminals wreaking havoc on U.S. currency. He said, "Do you know how hard this was for us to figure this out? I mean, how the hell did you do this?" He was intrigued by me, and it became a challenge for him and his team to figure out who was behind the counterfeiting that he, flatteringly, said was so good that they thought I was a big international cartel printing U.S. currency out of some shady country. To discover that I was a graphic artist with my own shop in Ogden, Utah was astonishing to them.

My lawyer was a guy who I will call Tom Laing Galveston, who was not a Mormon, and more than that, he was not everyone's cup of tea, shall we say. The day that we first went to meet the Secret Service in Salt Lake City, Tom Galveston was wearing a golf shirt and shorts. "I thought you guys were supposed to wear ties and suits and look professional!" I said to him, disappointed in my choice of lawyer already. Galveston said, "I want these guys to think I'm a country bumpkin."

He was also, shall we say, not a very helpful lawyer, as he didn't even try to talk me out of pleading guilty. Indeed, I almost thought he wanted to see me go to prison, such was his indifference to my lot.

I did get a little of my own back at my lawyer, though. Roger Rodak insisted that I surrender all of my existing counterfeit money and trusted me to do that. I was already cooperating with the Secret Service, and I was just a Utah Mormon guy like Roger, so why would he have thought that I might retain some of those Russ Swain $20s to pay my crummy lawyer?

So, I handed over about $150,000 in fake money to Roger Rodak, and the rest to Tom Laing Galveston, who never twigged to the fact that he had been paid with washed counterfeit money. I also inadvertently kept one of my $20s that I found years later stuffed in one of my shoes. I had put it there to be worn in as I walked around and so, to look "used" when produced. You saw a photo of that very bill in an earlier chapter.

Of course, not only did I want to plead guilty, but I had helped the Secret Service to find me guilty. They must have been watching me when I discarded the tools of my counterfeiting trade and saw me dispose of the evidence.

I had, in fact, found in my shop a sheet of Russ Swain $20s on which I had only printed one side. So, I burned the sheet, and then when it had burned down to the tiniest of pieces which I held between my thumb and forefinger, I threw that little piece of paper in a Coke can. Then I threw that Coke can into the dumpster behind the Empire waterbed store, far away from my shop. I mean, who is ever going to look inside of an empty Coke can? Nobody except the Secret Service, going through the counterfeiter's garbage with tweezers.

Roger told me that right up front. "We found a bill that was printed on one side and was burned except for the part where someone's thumb was holding it, which gave us a very, very clear indication of a thumbprint. That's rather incriminating, wouldn't you say?"

It shows how thorough the Secret Service can be when they go after something that they consider sacred, which is how they see American currency. The US Treasury estimates that there are between $70 to $200 million in counterfeit bills in circulation, with the $20 the most counterfeited bill in the USA, and the $100 bill the most counterfeited bill overseas. There is a lot of work for the Secret Service.

They charged me with the crime of conspiracy against the U.S. government, by blaspheming against the holy government money with my charlatan $20s, which would have brought down the government had it not been for some sharp eyed security guys in Vegas, and a ham-fisted money laundering printer and his Thanks to them, and U.S. penal code 18 § 473 which states "Whoever buys, sells, exchanges, transfers, receives, or delivers any false, forged, counterfeited, or altered obligation or other security of the United States, with the intent that the same be passed, published, or used as true and genuine, shall be fined under this title or imprisoned not more than 20 years." And I had made the counterfeit bills in question, so if you could get 20 years just for distributing them, I shuddered at what was coming my way. No matter how I looked at it, I was going to be in prison for a long time.

I did not dispute any part of the charge laid against me. Indeed, I wanted to get it all over with as fast as possible. My wife had come to my arraignment, but along with her and my lawyer, I was on my own. At my arraignment, when the charge is presented to you, you need to make a plea: guilty, or not. My diligent lawyer, Golf Shirt Galveston, had not prepared me, so when the judge asked me what my plea was, I said, "I'm guilty, your honor."

That's when Galveston suddenly remembered his professional obligations and corrected me, hissing loudly, "No, idiot, you're NOT guilty."

I turned to him, and said, in a clear and steady voice that the judge could hear, "I've confessed to the Feds, and I've handed over the $20 bills I printed on my own printing press. Now you expect me to lie to the guy who's going to sentence me?"

Galveston looked at me with his mouth open, like some slack jawed aging frat boy who was just told he had been uninvited to the party. The judge was amused, and rolled his eyes, smirking at Galveston as if he had just failed Courtroom Prep 101.

But, true to the weasel that he was, Galveston recovered,

and said, "Pardon me, your Honor, apparently my client did not understand the process."

I understood the process. He wanted me to plead not guilty so he could try to plea bargain for some kind of lesser sentence, and my current plea was depriving him of that legal pleasure.

So, I said, "I understand, your Honor. With all due respect, my attorney will decide my plea. I would rather you hear it from him than from me."

The Judge shook his head. "No, Mr. Swain. I need to hear it from you."

Galveston poked me in the ribs and hissed at me again. "Just say it! Tell him you're not guilty!"

I was embarrassed because this whole courtroom scene was even more counterfeit than my $20s, and everyone could see it. But I did as I was asked, and I told the Judge that I was "not guilty" and everyone was satisfied that justice, so far, was rolling along.

When Roger Rodak first interrogated me, he plowed through hundreds of questions. And I was cooperative. At the end of the interrogation, he said, "I'm impressed. Fifty percent of the questions that I asked you, I already knew the answer to, and you told me the truth. And I appreciate that, because if there's one thing that I just despise, it's when somebody lies to me."

Roger wanted me to show him how I had done it, as he was fascinated by the quality of my Russ Swain $20s, so I showed him. He was intrigued by the whole thing because it had been such a challenge for the Secret Service to figure it out. He wanted to see how I had done it, so I took him on a tour of Para Graphics. He was a keen student, and because I had been cooperative, they did not need to dismantle my shop. I showed him the paper, and the ink, and told him about the diamond dust, and he was clearly impressed. He told me that if we weren't on opposite sides of the case, we'd likely be friends. In the end, we were friends, I like to think.

I did not tell Roger about Tommy, as there was no point, and Tommy was dead. I just told him that I had lost a job, had debt, so this was my creative solution. At the end of my counterfeiting lesson, Roger turned to me with a grin. He told me that if I had used a numbering machine, they likely never would have caught me. My bills were that good. Then he shook my hand and for a heartbeat, I wanted to ask him where I could have bought that numbering machine, but my better angel told me to just smile, and silently return the firm handshake.

In fact, my Russ Swain $20s were so good that I am responsible for changes made to the design of U.S. currency to make it much more difficult to counterfeit. Of course, counterfeiting still happens, but today's currency, with all its colored bits and watermarks, means that I wouldn't know where to start. You would need some serious technology to pull it off, and I have no interest in going down that road again.

But I did have to go down the road to Salt Lake City for my trial. There had been a story in one of the newspapers about me and I was shocked to see it, not thinking myself newsworthy My kids suddenly weren't invited to play at the homes of some of their friends, and my wife was regarded as the counterfeiter's spouse, but the Church at least kept her close.

And though she said we would get through it I was worried now that she would not. But I had made it clear to Roger and the Secret Service that I was a lone gunman, so to speak. No one in my family, or my wife's family, knew anything about it. Indeed, my own in-laws had provided evidence of my guilt. John the Printer, and his wife Carrie, might have talked but I do not know. I have not spoken to them since.

I put on a suit and tie to convey the fair-haired Mormon boy as best as I could, and drove to Salt Lake City with my wife, pretty much in silence. We both knew that this might be our last ride down the I-15 for a while. If the prosecution threw the book at me and the judge accepted it, I could be in prison for maybe twenty years.

The federal court in Salt Lake City is a big gray building that looks windowless, but the windows are disguised in the design. To me, glancing up at it as we entered, it already looked like a prison. The fact that it was a couple of blocks down from Temple Square, where the great Mormon temple sits, was not lost on my wife, nor on me. I had betrayed a core tenet of my faith: do not transgress the Bible, which says thou shalt not steal. I had stolen from the U.S. government. But Christianity also allows for redemption and forgiveness. Maybe one day, I thought, as I walked into court to accept my fate, I would find that redemption. Maybe one day, I would find a different kind of diamond dust.

My golf shirted lawyer Tom Galveston had prepared me for prison life and seemed to enjoy himself in doing so. He told me the kind of place where I would be dispatched would be like a country club, with tennis courts and weight rooms and comfortable quarters. "Club Fed", he called it. I called it prison. I worried that if it had a golf course, then this skeevy guy might even come to visit the client for whom he had done nothing much at all to stop landing there, just to play a round of golf in his golf shirt.

The prosecutor was an older guy, more than 60 years old, with wispy gray hair. Behind his gold rim spectacles, his eyes were cold and unfeeling. He seemed highly intelligent, but it was the kind of intelligence to grasp facts and figures, and not what made people tick. His emotional intelligence IQ was about zero.

And he wanted to win by putting me in prison for a long time. He was pressing his case to the maximum, and he paced in front of the Judge like justice in motion, stopping only to glare at me in rage. He flashed pictures of my money and cast his disgusted eyes on them as well, all the while making me seem like some evil criminal mastermind out to ruin the country.

"The quality of these bills is extraordinary," he practically shouted. "Mr. Swain meant to do this money fakery for a long time, and he meant to defraud the American people for a long time. This was no hobby. This was done with criminal intent. This counterfeiter stole from the American people, and from the U.S. government. He is guilty of conspiracy against the U.S. government, and he should receive the maximum sentence possible under our law."

I thought I was done for, but it was at that point something that I could never have dreamed would happen, happened. Secret Service Agent Roger Rodak leapt to his feet in the courtroom, his cheeks flushed, and with anger in his voice, he began to defend me.

"Your Honor, during the course of my investigation, I have become very well acquainted with Mr. Swain. He never once lied to me about what he did. And what he did doesn't show criminal intent. It shows creative intent. Mr. Swain is a very creative guy. Mr. Swain is not a criminal! He's an artist!"

And of a sudden, Roger Rodak had become my defense attorney, saying that he disagreed completely with what the prosecution was arguing and invoking me as a true artist. The prosecutor looked at Roger as if he had just committed the greatest injustice he had ever seen, but then he looked at the Judge, and saw that the Judge did not agree with him. He was interested in what Roger had to say.

The Judge was an older Mormon guy who looked like every Mormon church elder I had ever seen, full of rectitude and gravitas, and he was listening intently to this Secret Service agent arguing my case, and who had way more credibility in this courtroom than my attorney had. Golf Shirt Galveston was smart enough to sit down and shut up and let Agent Rodak defend me.

When Roger had finished, the judge thanked him. "That's very interesting, Agent Rodak. Thank you. Would you be okay, then, if we gave Mr. Swain a suspended sentence?"

"I think that would be justice, your Honor."

The prosecutor looked as if Roger had just stabbed him through his cruel and vengeful little heart.

And the Judge didn't care. He gave me a Biblically appropriate seven years of probation, with the order that I had to buy back all the counterfeit $20 bills I had spent.

"How am I to do that, your Honor?" I asked. "With respect, I don't have the resources right now. Could you set me up on a payment program?"

The judge smiled at me and said, "The payment program would be this: as the Secret Service gathers up the counterfeit bills, you have to buy them back from the Secret Service."

I didn't quite understand the gesture at the time, but I thought it was going to be hard for the Secret Service to find my Russ Swain $20s. I saw Roger after the first week and asked him "Well, have you got any 20s for me to buy back?

"No," he said. It was the same thing a month later, at which time I was beginning to feel curious. Roger explained a little. "You should take this as a compliment! It's hard for us to find your money." I didn't quite understand the gesture at the time, but I came to realize that it was going to be impossible for the Secret Service to find my Russ Swain $20s. Forty years later, I've never had to buy a bill back, because they're still out there circulating, just like "real" money.

It does give one pause, though, to wonder what the Feds did with that hefty chunk of Russ Swain $20s. I mean, the perpetrator had been caught and convicted, and the Secret Servicemen were given the task of rounding-up the bills that were put in circulation.

I'm surprised that one of them didn't find some gangster he knew and say, "Give me fifty grand for this $150 thousand" that I had turned into them. Then, any money that the guy spent, if he got caught, would be blamed back on the guy who was known to have printed them in the first place. The Feds could have gained points for finding some of those bills that were circulating, and I would have had to buy them back.

But Roger Rodak was a standup guy, who was very religious and not the kind to give in to that kind of temptation. I think that a similar scenario in today's political climate would have seen those bills passing between the hands of the good-old-boys, with them saying, "Don't spill the margaritas!" as they handed my fake money to all and sundry.

Roger had also told me, over a glass of lemonade, as we had become friends, that I had received several letters of support from community members, including one from a high-ranking Mormon that carried a lot of weight with the Judge. Now, if I had written that letter to the Judge on behalf of a high-ranking Mormon, what would I have said about myself? I often wonder about that.

I walked out of the court and into the Salt Lake City summer sun as if a great weight had been lifted from me. I also knew that what I had done, despite the fact I was not locked up in prison, still had to be dealt with in my family. I realized that I could get on with my life, but it was not the same life that I had before because now there was a great giant hole in it.

My wife had realized that I was not the man she thought she had married, and she was going to have a nice little middle of the road Mormon life with me. I had not left her alone as a single parent to look after two young daughters while I did my prison time. The fact that I was still here, still with them, created a whole new set of problems, including the strain with my daughters' maternal grandparents, who were the first to learn of my guilt.

My wife was just very, very quiet. I remember lying in bed that night and trying to talk about it and she just said, "I don't want to talk." She turned over and turned out the light. That light going out left me in the dark, literally, and figuratively. I had seen justice deliver an unexpected reality to me earlier that day. I had expected to be shackled and *en route* to prison, but instead I was lying in bed with my wife, who no longer saw me as her husband.

I had always had a plan to get out of jams, from childhood to now. I had written notes for my classmates and faked report cards, I had painted a postage stamp so real it had got me a job, and I had created $20 bills that were so good that even the Secret Service congratulated me. But I had no plan for this situation I was in now, with the light of the truth beaming down on my every breathing moment, except to try to live the cleanest life I could possibly live, forever and ever, amen. Of course, as the saying goes, the road to hell is paved with good intentions. And before too long, I would be back on that road.

8

A Test
and
A Reckoning

I was not in prison, at least not in one run by the Feds, but I was in a prison of my own making in my very own home. I had put my wife through an extraordinary process, in which she discovered I had lied to her. I was not at all the man she knew- the good Mormon and talented printer with the booming business. It was a counterfeit, even a good one, but nonetheless, it was a dark reality that I had created, and now had to admit to those I loved the most. Indeed, the consequences of that lie could have seen her become a single parent with two young daughters, while I wiled away the years in Club Fed. She had told our daughters that I had some legal difficulties, but no more than that. How they didn't know more than that I can say owes much to the Mormons who are not gossips. They circled the wagons to protect my girls. My wife asked me not to discuss it with them. Ever. Which was fine with me. I mean, what could I tell them to make it all seem like a good thing?

My wife knew what she was up against no matter which way the court case against me went. The stress of her reality was coming into clearer focus now that my own stress of going to prison had been relieved by my probation. But I still had to live with my family, and live in Ogden, and get on with my life.

I kept my head down, and did not see anyone, really, except my family and my mother, who did not, thankfully, keep reminding me of my crime. She told me to use this new start to do good for the world. I promised I would, and I promised myself that I would not even jaywalk going forward. I was not going to seek out John and ask him if he had given me up. He and his wife also received suspended sentences, as they couldn't actually jail them if they hadn't jailed me. So, I was happy, in a contrite way, about that.

had always been captivated by Plato's famous allegory of the cave, written around 380 BCE, which is one of the most important passages in his book *The Republic*. In it, Socrates speaks to Plato's brother Glaukon about captives in a cave, who are chained up, and unable to turn around. They are forced to stare at a cave wall. Their brutal reality is provided by objects and noises behind them that their captors manipulate to become shadows on the wall thanks to the fires which burn within the cave. These captives, knowing only that reality, think the shadows define their reality. Socrates explains to Plato's brother that we all resemble captives who are chained deep within a cavern, who do not yet realize that there is more to reality than the shadows we see against the wall.

I felt very much like that captive in the cave, the difference being that I was the one who set the fire to produce the shadows now tormenting me. My wife had moved from shock to anger, seasoned with humiliation. She was not throwing china at me, or my clothes out the window, or anything like that. She was just so very hurt. How could she show up at church on Sunday with me and the kids and not be scorned as the wife of this criminal, the man who lied to her and betrayed her trust and used her goodness against her?

Oddly, the answer to that was surprising. I discovered a new layer of reality about the world around me. While you might be inclined to think the world was looking at the big scarlet "C-for-Counterfeiter" splashed on my forehead, they were not. People have their own lives and their own problems, and they didn't have time or the inclination to look harshly at me. They just regarded me as a loose cannon, and let it go. So, I really didn't deal with a lot of social estrangement from friends or from people who kind of knew me from my business. It was a comfort, albeit a small one, as my estrangement from my wife was growing, and, I feared, past the point of no return. She had said we would get through it. But now, it was increasingly apparent that she would not, and so we would not.

So, I did that classic evasive thing and plunged myself back into work. I would spend fourteen hours a day in Para Graphics. The office was unchanged, but my business card boxes were gone. Roger Rodak and his team had them and their contents. My clients came back, and I made brochures and posters and letterheads and t-shirt designs, so I was very busy. In a way, my wife was indeed that single parent she feared becoming since I was out of the house at 6 AM and not back until 8 PM. I was trying to get as much honest work done as I could do to pay our bills and stay out of trouble.

And then, one day, trouble walked in the door. He was a white guy, about forty years old, and looked like a man who had seen some living, but not in any dangerous way. He was dressed casually, in a leather jacket and jeans, and he gave off a street-smart vibe, in how he carried himself. His head swiveled around my shop to check it out, as if to make sure no ears were listening in as he made his pitch. I soon saw why.

He told me that he was a cop who had been working vice

in Las Vegas, dealing with whatever constitutes a vice crime in a city seemingly built on vice. I felt a chill run up my spine. John the Printer and his very ordinary wife had been busted in Vegas. Could the Vegas cops now have something on me that Roger had missed?

The Vegas cop's voice was calm and steady, his brown eyes unblinking as he went in a direction I had not expected and could never have imagined. He told me that in his experience as a cop, you had the chance to work on both sides of the street, as it were. Enforcing the law, or breaking it.

"Your problem, Mr. Swain," he began, a beginning which rattled me by both the fact that he thought I had a problem that prevented me from a successful life of crime, and that he knew my name, "was that you had the wrong partner when you were making your $20s. They were of pretty high quality, if I do say so."

When I heard that I wondered if he knew Roger. Surely, Roger would never consort with a cop criminal, but maybe this guy had somehow got hold of Roger's intel. You have to remember that there was no Google yet, so he could not have just looked me up online. And no Vegas reporters had come asking me how I had done it. He had to have inside knowledge.

"So, Mr. Swain, I am offering you a sweet deal. Keep doing what you're so good at doing, and I will be your partner. We'll make a lot of money, more than you ever dreamed possible. I mean, I know how to do it. I'm a cop."

I was stunned. I had never seen him around Ogden, but then I did not know everyone in town. Still, he seemed like a guy from out of town. Maybe he had been sent by that vindictive prosecutor in my trial, who hated the fact I had been given probation. Yes, that's what it was. Maybe this was a test, to see if my public remorse, which I had expressed in court for what I had done, was the real thing. To see if they could entrap me and lock me up in some dank prison. There was only one response I could make to his offer.

"I think you should leave this shop immediately, sir," I said, as I walked briskly to the front door and opened it for him.

He didn't say anything until he reached the door, then looked at me, still unblinking, and he said, "You sure about this, Swain? We could make a fortune together."

"I'm as sure about that as I am sure that the sun rises just over there," I said, pointing to the east. "Good day to you."

I did not watch him get into his car, so I don't know if it had Vegas plates, or if it had U.S. Government plates. I was shaking with a mixture of fear and anger that I had been so nakedly tested by whomever had sent him.

Or maybe it wasn't a test. Maybe he really was who he said he was and had heard through the cop grapevine about my Russ Swain $20s, and he saw a rich opportunity. No matter if this proposed reality was a test by the law, or a temptation from a crooked cop, I was not having any of it. I was never going to be on the wrong side of a courtroom again. Besides, I had promised my wife that I would never break the law again. If I did, she said she would divorce me. I was more afraid of losing her and my daughters than I was of the law.

And as it happened, I already had more trouble with the law, in the form of the Ogden police department. Once upon a time I was the guy they turned to when they needed beautiful hand lettering on their police cars, back in the day before decals. I would devote my entire Saturday when I was in college to writing "We serve and protect" on the side of their cars, along with POLICE. Now, the Ogden police saw me as a target. Or at least one of them did.

Chip looked like a California surfer dude who was tall, fit, with a full head of blonde hair, and clean-cut. That also describes your average ideal Nazi, so take your pick. He wasn't violent, but he was persistent. In fact, he just wouldn't leave me alone.

Indeed, Chip was an apt moniker due to the sizable chip that he wore on his shoulder after learning that Public Enemy Number One had been caught by the Feds for crimes committed in the city that he had sworn to protect, and then, shockingly, I was released. When he first heard about me and my Russ Swain $20s, Chip would drive by the house and the studio. He would even tail me on the road hoping to give me a speeding ticket or wait for me to jaywalk—which I had sworn never to do. It ate at him that I was still at large, pushing my thumb into the eye of the law.

Once he even pulled me over with his lights flashing and siren blaring, which startled the heck out of me. I had a little alarm in my shop that had gone off because some fumes had set off the smoke detector. So, Chip came full blast after me to pull me over and ask if I was burning more fake money.

He was really antagonistic toward me. It felt like he was stalking me, his head swirling with his mission: *I've got a criminal living right here in Riverdale, and I am going to catch him.*

Every day, as he patrolled the mean streets of Riverdale, Utah (mean in the sense that some kid might snatch some candy from a convenience store shelf, or some scofflaw might jaywalk) he would make it a point to drive through the narrow corridor that separated the two parallel strip malls— one of which housed my business, Para Graphics. Just so that I could see he was there. A blizzard would whip around inside my gut when I would see him out there, knowing that he thought he could do whatever he wanted, and so, he just might.

On one occasion, I was working alone in the back of the shop when the little buzzer alerted me that a customer had come through the front door. I emerged to greet the customer and there stood Chip with his sidearm aimed at me, steadying it with both hands, arms straight out.

"Hey Chip, what's up?" I said as calmly as I could, with that blizzard swirling in my stomach. I knew he was probably thinking he could shoot me and claim it was a suicide. The cops would circle the wagons and say, "Yep. Swain couldn't live with what he had done. Killed himself with a gunshot at twenty paces."

I didn't move from where I stood, and Chip kept his pistol aimed at me. "What's going on in here, Swain?" he growled.

"Nothing that would warrant you waving a gun around," I said with as much reason as I could muster. And then I felt compelled to add: "Even my worst clients don't get that threatening, when their deadlines are looming."

Chip blinked at that. Had I just insulted him? He wasn't sure, and he didn't holster the pistol. "Well, somebody's emergency alarm is going off and the station sent me to investigate. Mind if I take a look around in the back?"

I just couldn't resist a sarcastic comeback, "You got a warrant, cowboy?" The expression that flashed in his blue eyes was one of pure contempt. He really looked like he wanted to shoot me.

"Chip, Chip! I'm only messing with you! Of course, you can look around. Make yourself at home! Look—both hands, right where you can see 'em. Just relax and do whatever it is you do, and I'll stay out of your way."

He lowered his pistol and walked around the small production area. He checked out a sketch lying on my worktable of my new project for Morris Travel, which was entitled "Everyone Wants to Escape—Here's How!" It was a mock-up for their winter vacation brochure, but I am sure Chip thought it was some "How To" manual I was making to sell to people inside prisons. After poking around, looking under tables and inside the printing press, he was certain there was nothing there that could be considered "unusual" and that I wasn't pumping out more counterfeit currency. It was only then that he re-holstered his gun as he walked to the door. Then he turned to me and said in his best bad TV show cop voice, "I've got my eye on you, Swain."

Then he left.

I may not have been committing any crimes, but by constantly focusing on design problems or print deadlines, there were details of a legal nature that I had pushed aside. My own procrastination would give Chip his chance to send me up the river.

One such detail was getting the safety-inspection updated on my car. Back in those days, we had a sticker placed on the lower left-hand side of the windshield which indicated the month the sticker had expired. Chip must have noticed that my sticker would soon expire. I had many other things on my mind besides my car sticker.

He lay in wait for me to pull out of my parking space and onto the public thoroughfare with that expired sticker. I drove out to get myself lunch, and within seconds the flashing lights of his cop car were behind me, letting me know Chip was on to something criminal that I did not know about.

I assumed he'd want to see my license and I reached around for my wallet, but he had his gun in hand again as he demanded, "Outta the car Swain, now! Keep your hands where I can see 'em!" I could see pedestrians looking at me in alarm. One mother pulled her two young children into a lingerie shop for safety. I was clearly a dangerous man.

"Okay, okay," I said, getting out of the car with my hands in front of me, not clutching any leftover Russ Swain $20s. I was surprised by hostility, excessive even for him, and added "no need to get all 'Rambo' on me. What's this about?"

He looked at me like I was a child murderer and said, "You're driving an unsafe vehicle!" Then he holstered his gun. "Now turn and face the car and place both hands behind your back!"

With that he handcuffed me and did his best rendition of my Miranda rights. "You're a menace to this community, Swain, and now you're going to jail!"

That was it. A tow truck came and impounded my car.

The woman came out of the lingerie shop where she had taken refuge with her children and gave me a look of such venomous scorn that I felt for the kids. I nodded to the kids and smiled to assure them that I was a good person and maybe Mr. Policeman was an idiot, then Chip put a hand on my head and shoved me into the back seat of his cruiser and drove me to the "steel hotel." I said nothing on the way, as I found Chip's actions so petty, excessive, and bizarre that I knew reason would not be welcome here. It would prevail once I got to the police station.

It did not. The cops at the station inked-up my fingers to take my prints, then they took a mugshot, and told me I could make my solitary phone call. I took a deep breath and called my wife who was working as the in-house designer for a travel agency in Salt Lake. I never really thought about calling anyone else, and I figured that this was one crime call that would not upset her. I could hear her eyes roll over the phone as I told her that I needed $500 to be bailed out. I told her there was no rush and that she could finish her work shift, as I wasn't going anywhere. There was a long pause, and then she sighed, and said, to my great relief, that she was on it. She would bail me out.

I settled into my holding cell and became aware that the eyes of my cell mate were upon me. He was a hulking guy who looked like he had been sired by first cousins, with eyes like death. "What're you in for?" he inquired.

"Uh, it's a sticker thing—kinda complicated. You?"

"Rape," he said, flatly.

We ended the conversation there.

After about forty minutes of silence in the cell, a jail guard called out to me. "Inmate Swain? You've got a phone call."

The cop led me to a window and handed me the phone receiver. I had no idea who was calling but I picked up the phone and, given the ridiculousness of putting me in a cell with an accused rapist for having an expired sticker on my car, I tried to make light of things, and barked into the phone, "I told you never to call me here!"

Chip was on the other end. "You're some kind of smart ass," he told me. "I've been ordered by my higher-ups to release you with a ticket to be paid before ten days have passed. But know this—if you so much as spit on a sidewalk, I'll be coming for you. I'll be coming for you!"

With that, he hung up. I was still holding the phone, aware that the other officers present were unaware that our conversation had ended, and they were listening to my response. So, I stated very clearly, "That's very flattering Chip, really. But as I've told you repeatedly, I only date women!"

Everybody started shuffling papers and getting back to work. I had made my point. As for Chip, I could understand why he'd want to be a cop—in his uniform he had impunity, and his righteous rage could run wild as he protected the good people of Ogden from expired auto sticker guys like me. But I could never understand what kind of insecurities he suffered to want to use his power of authority in such a stupidly bullying manner.

Since I was once again dealing with the law, it may not surprise you to learn that I did have one more court to contend with, and I knew that my chances of keeping the faith, so to speak, were not on my side.

In the Church of Jesus Christ of Latter-day Saints, a process exists for removing members who have transgressed from the Church rolls. Your name is taken off the list, and just like that you are off the bus heading to heaven.

The process of being removed from the rolls of the LDS Church is not an arbitrary process, but a formal one, and structured very much like a court of law. I received a letter, as I knew I would, informing me of the time and date of my disciplinary hearing, and so I went, knowing that just like in the Federal courtroom, there was not much I could say in my defense.

My wife was more hurt by it than I was, and finally it was something the girls knew about. It was a church thing that was by no means common, but the church spoke loudly to the community. They looked at me with sympathetic curiosity, as if their dear old dad had not absorbed the lessons on faith that they knew so well. I had failed the life exam.

Even so, Mormon excommunication was pretty enlightened. In 1834, Joseph Smith, who was the prophet of the newly formed Church of Jesus Christ of Latter-day Saints, received a revelation to protect the rights of the accused during church disciplinary procedures.

After the American Revolution, the new country embraced the idea of individual rights, both in religion and government. Smith was a man of his time, and also took care to make sure that the accused had rights. He put those protections in Latter-day Saints scripture known as the Doctrine and Covenants. As Smith established just what would happen to members of the church who found themselves in disciplinary procedures, he organized a "High Council" to judge members who disobeyed church doctrine. The council was made up of high-ranking male church officials, and it was to present "evidence" on both sides of cases with "equity and justice."

I did not have to face a High Council or Quorum of Twelve who were to judge me as a worthy, or unworthy member of the church. Instead, I had to go to the Stake President's office in the Stake-Center Chapel in Ogden for my "trial."

I wore my Sunday best, of course, and walked in calmly and alone to the room where I would be judged. I could not ask my wife to come to this court. Indeed, we were close to the point where we could not even call ourselves married.

So, I walked in by myself to face my twelve judges, all in jackets and ties, who were seated six a side around a large conference table. These gentlemen who were weighing my fate asked me questions about what I was thinking when I so blatantly transgressed the laws of the Church, but I had no desire to expand on my very simple statement. I told them I was guilty.

The tribunal only lasted for about an hour, and while this LDS court allowed someone chosen by lot to speak on my behalf, the only thing he could say was that I was a nice counterfeiter. It was all just a formality.

A few days later, I received the next letter from HQ confirming what I already knew. It confirmed that the excommunication court had taken place and that "Russell Swain would no longer have his name recorded in the rolls of the church."

What that meant was that I could still go to church, but I just couldn't participate. So, for the sake of my wife and children, I stayed away. The last thing that they needed to see was me doing nothing in church on a Sunday. Just sitting there, watching everyone else worship.

So, another way of seeing the world had just changed for me. I had been the fair-haired Mormon boy since I was born in that can of pork and beans. I was my mother's angel baby, raised in the Church by her, and I had freely gone on a mission to proclaim the faith to the people of Brazil. I held to the tenets of my faith, and did not drink alcohol or caffeine, and I was devoted to my family.

Of course, I had lied to my wife about counterfeiting money, to which I had plead guilty in a court of law. And that undid everything. Did I still believe in a divine being who was looking out for me? Or did I believe that was just some larger shadow on the cave, lit from the fires of our own hells?

I did not know. A few years later, I would, as the Mormon faith allows, proclaim my redemption, and ask to be let back inside the tent. They said yes, and so I was baptized back into the Mormon church. I had mainly done this out of a desperate attempt to save my marriage, but my wife divorced me. Our marriage had been ending ever since the truth of what I had done had become public, and while she had tried her best to see it through, the man she saw was not the man she married. Her reality of me had changed, and I had to go.

Para Graphics went, too. Once Steve Jobs had worked out that computer thing in his garage, everyone with an Apple, or a PC, could be a graphic designer. They did not need me.

I also concluded that the Mormon faith would be better off without me as well. After they so graciously let me return, I went to church for a while, and I really tried to be a good Mormon.

But I knew that I did not want to go through another excommunication court, and while I still maintained a deep respect for my faith and was grateful for its influence, it was time for me to quietly tiptoe away.

There were some things in my life that I did not think contributed to the tenets of the faith to which I had been readmitted. I had taken to drinking Mormon meth, which the world knows as coffee. Now and then, I took a sip from a glass of wine with a client or a friend, though I will admit that wine has a tendency to loosen the screws of one's focus. I don't think I could have pulled off my $20s if I had been tippling from a bottle of Italian red.

And now, I was also counterfeiting paintings.

Like Hemingway's famous notion of how people go bankrupt, slowly, then all at once, it was a bit like that with me. Over the years, since I had painted that moose on the cabin wall at Island Park, I had been helping friends with their redecoration of their homes and other recreational properties, and word had spread that I was not too bad at painting murals, or doing trompe l'oeil work, a French term that literally means "to fool the eye."

It's an optical illusion to make you think you are seeing something that you are not. In his work, *Natural History*,

Pliny the Elder describes a painting competition between two artists to determine which one of them is the better artist.

In Pliny's story, the artist Zeuxis unveils his work. He has painted grapes so lifelike that birds fly down to attempt to eat them. When trying to unveil the painting by the artist Parhassius, they thought that the curtains which were hiding the work were in fact the painting. Zeuxis admits defeat, proclaiming that it is one thing to fool an animal but another to fool man. That's what trompe l'oeil does.

It was right up my alley, connecting back to those report cards I had concocted in high school, and that postage stamp I had copied which got me the advertising agency job, and those counterfeit $20s which had gotten me out of trouble with Tommy the Shark, and into trouble with the law and my wife and her parents.

However, before my painting career took off, I once again found myself in a courtroom, and once again my wife was there. And once again it had happened because I was trying to carry on the spirit of Warren, long since gone to the great pick-up truck repository, and do a good thing for someone by changing their reality.

After the dissolution of my marriage and shuttering of my business, I found refuge in decorative painting, doing this on the walls of wealthy people's homes. Marketing that kind of work is dependent upon building networks of clients and word-of-mouth referrals. I was fortunate in that I had acquired a substantial amount of work.

I was approached by a young, out-of-work house painter, looking for a job, whom I will call Mac. He was a slender guy in his early twenties, with a great flop of brown hair that hid one of his eyes, which should have been my clue. He would do all the prep-work, such as masking and priming, and he was eager to sharpen his skills. I explained that I wasn't looking for that kind of help but that I could offer him temporary employment on a large job that I was anxious to finish.

Mac was bereft of any hard currency and struggled to get to work on time because he was living with his single mother, and they shared a car. They took turns dropping each other at their prospective jobs. Mac and his mom were struggling to get by and at the end of the job he worked on with me, I offered to extend some help.

Now that Warren had departed, my work vehicle was an older model Jeep Cherokee. It had high miles on its engine, but it ran well. I referred Mac to another painting contractor for work, and to further help him, I "gifted" him my Jeep, hoping it would give him and his mother some relief in their transportation struggle. All I asked in return was that he honor my gesture by taking care to immediately register the vehicle in his name, and toss the old plates, to avoid any issues of liability. He assured me that he would.

I wished him well and we went our separate ways. But not for long, because Mac was a weasel.

A couple of months later, I landed a job in the home of a couple who defined the term "socialites." Lots of money, and taste. I was referred to them by an interior designer as my work had risen up the artistic food chain, and so, I would discover, did the opportunities. We all hit it off and became fast friends. Half-way through the job, they had house guests —a couple of well-heeled Frenchmen whom they had met in Paris on a biking tour and who loved the complex *faux* finish work I had developed for their home. *Faux* finish is a painting technique that creates texture and nuance by replicating the look or feel of other surfaces. Like making a flat wooden surface look like marble.

They asked if I would consider going to Paris to create a *faux* finish in their home. *Mais oui!* I wanted to go to Paris! My socialite friends would come too, and we would all make magic in the City of Light. My trip was immediately arranged and would all be paid for, and I would stay at their home that I was going to help "restore." All I had to do was acquire a passport.

In order to do that I needed to produce ID, and I discovered that I had lost my driver's license. It had been at least a couple of months since I'd seen it. I had been so busy that I had not taken the time to really look hard for it, but once I did, and could not find it, I needed to get a new one, spurred on by my Paris adventure. I went immediately to the Department of Motor Vehicles with my alternate ID and applied for a driver's license.

A very lovely lady who was working at the station was looking at my records and she leaned towards me and whispered, "You seem like such a nice man, I'm going to let you just walk out of here and I won't mention to anyone that you came in. But you'd better leave!"

I was astonished. Why was she asking me to go when I hadn't got what I came for?

"I don't think you understand," I said. "I need a driver's license!"

"*You* don't understand," she countered. "There's a warrant for your arrest for two DUI's and failure-to-appear. Your driving privileges have automatically been revoked! I can't give you a driver's license in any way, shape, or form."

I was shocked. Not only did I barely drink alcohol, as a hanging-on-by-my-fingernails Mormon, I argued that I had a perfect driving record, with no tickets or points. She pulled up the dates on her monitor. I had been positively ID'd by the officer who pulled me over driving a white Jeep Cherokee, registered to me. I had shown him my driver's license, signed the ticket promising to appear in court, and then I had ignored all subsequent notices and warnings. Apparently, this had happened twice, and so the authorities had produced a bench warrant to have me jailed.

"Mac!!" I thought, "You little bastard!" I went home and rummaged to find his number.

It transpired that Mac had taken the Jeep that I had given him and made a quick sale to someone whom he didn't know for cash, and then had let him drive away with my plates. The new driver, who was about my age and complexion, found my driver's license under the seat and had presented it whenever he was pulled over. It was his lucky day!

The tickets were sent to my old address where I no longer lived, and no one was the wiser, me included. I was screwed! How could I get out of this jam? And how could I get a passport and get to Paris? Time was running out and I had to clear my name.

I called the courts, and they set up a court date in Salt Lake City, assuring me that the arresting officer would be present so I could clear myself. I showed up, and explained my predicament to the Judge, but the officer who could identify me had some kind of an emergency to attend to and he didn't show.

So, they arranged another court date for me for the following week. But before I left, the Judge felt compelled to reprimand me, saying that if the officer positively identified me as this DUI scofflaw, it wouldn't bode well. But I was allowed to leave.

I had mentioned my predicament to my daughters who, in turn, explained it to their mother. They all lived in our cottage house in the East Bench, and the girls were now in Middle School. We were all on good terms, and my daughters were concerned about my latest legal dilemma. The poor dears were probably just trying to prevent their surname "Swain" from becoming synonymous with "criminal" in Utah.

A day before I was due in court, my wife was driving along in downtown Ogden to buy a custom piece of glass for a picture frame, at a glass store. The only place she could find to park was directly behind a white Jeep Cherokee that was parked in front of a Mexican restaurant. She recognized it as my old Jeep, due to the paint splatters on the tailgate.

So, she immediately called the police department who

sent an officer. As if by divine providence, the officer was someone with whom she and I were both well acquainted, a brother-in-law to our good friends. She explained the situation and they both agreed to wait until the driver emerged from the restaurant. When he came forth, the cop, trying to suppress a grin, asked, "Is this your car?"

"Yes officer, it is. Is there a problem?"

"Just a routine question, but may I see your driver's license?"

"Certainly." And the guy handed him my license. The officer studied his face and the photo on the license. We looked quite a bit alike. Then the cop pulled out his ace card. "Let me ask you, Mr. Swain, Do you recognize this lovely lady here?"

The man looked at my wife and furrowed his brow. "Can't say as I do."

"Hmmm... that's odd," said the cop. "Because this lady, with whom I am well acquainted, insists that she was married to the owner of this Jeep, who coincidentally has the same name as you, for twenty-two years. Odd that you wouldn't remember her. Please place your hands behind you. You have the right to remain silent..."

My wife explained details of my impending court date to the officer and asked if he would give her a statement in writing that she would in turn give to me, to take to court. He did so with great pleasure.

The following day, I appeared in court, feeling confident that the wheels of justice would turn in my direction. The judge asked me how I would plead, and this time, I got to say loudly and truly: "Not guilty."

He in turn asked the police officer if I was the same person to whom was issued the citation. "Yes, your honor."

"Are you sure?" he asked.

"Without a doubt," your honor.

The Judge turned to me and asked, "What do you have to say in response?"

"If it please the court, your honor, I have a document here that I wish to present. May I approach the bench?"

As the Judge read my letter, a look of contempt drew across his face as he turned to the officer. He told him, bluntly and clearly, that if he were ever to appear and testify in his courtroom again without getting his facts straight that he would hold him accountable and in contempt of court. He then ordered him out of the courtroom.

He turned to me and said those sweet legal words, "Mr. Swain, you're free to go."

And I went to Paris. It was that trip that was filled with such inspiration and learning, that before too long, it would lead me to create my first Picasso.

9

My Picassos

I went to France to launch a new level in my life as an artist, one which would see me pick up the brush again, and paint. I had never been to Europe, only ever having been as far as Brazil and Mexico, which was a long time ago. And when I landed in Paris, the City of Light, all she had to do was wink a little of her magical light at me and like so many before me, I was in love.

The sights and tastes were more than I had imagined, with a simple fresh baguette and a touch of butter somehow seeming gourmet, and every Parisian seeming to be on their way to a fashion show, in which they were the star.

The thing that inspired me most was indeed the light of Paris, a light that had inspired so many artists. It was as if the sky, even when gray, was lush and luminous in a different way than I was used to seeing. The moisture in the air of Paris gave the light a liquid quality that just dazzled me.

I stayed for a couple of days in the apartment belonging to my Paris friends, who also changed my reality. One of them was originally from Australia, and he served in the Australian embassy in Paris. The other was a flight attendant. They were a couple of gay guys, and at the time, I had never been exposed to anybody who was gay.

They were so likable and kind and just wonderful guys. And so, it occurred to me: why would I care about who someone chooses to love? I'd never stopped to think about that as an issue, or how I felt about it until I was living in the middle of it in Paris, and now that I had done, it was just fine. So, my view of reality had been changed by them.

So, too, was my view of art. I inhaled the museums of Paris, seeing that enigmatic smile on the Mona Lisa at the Louvre made me connect with Da Vinci, and seeing the invention of modern art on display at the National Museum of Modern Art at the Centre Pompidou connected me to a whole generation of artists who wanted to change the way we saw.

Of course, the museum that I loved the most was the Picasso, housed in a mansion built in the 17th century for a tax collector who got rich collecting a tax on salt. I loved the museum because in it, I saw Picasso's early work as an artist, which revealed his great technical ability to represent things as they looked. Even his first self-portrait at the age of 15, in 1896, is astonishing: his facial features are balanced and in true to life colors, while the shadows around him are pronounced, showing a dark self-knowledge already present —which is, I think, the mark of early genius.

And as I walked through the museum, I saw how Picasso's view of reality changed as he explored the creative possibilities of Cubism. Ten years after he painted the self-portrait at the top, he painted a new self-portrait.

Picasso's view of his own reality had changed, and he showed the world how. Picasso challenged the so-called "traditional way" of painting reality as everyone saw it (i.e.

an apple is an apple and not a dog) and wanted to help create a new way of seeing that reflected the 20th century. This artistic revolution was called Cubism.

Cubism offered a new way to represent reality which began in 1907, with Pablo Picasso and other artists leading the way. Cubism involves different ways of seeing, or perceiving, the world around us. So, Cubists offered us different views of a single subject in the same picture, as they thought that we do not look at something from just one angle, but from many angles as we change our position, and so, as we change our perspective. Cubism became a different way to see the realities around us.

So, I saw in that museum that Picasso didn't begin his life as an artist by painting people with noses that bent 90 degrees to the left. But he evolved to one who saw that reality as more accurate to how we look at things. And, of course, his journey made him one of history's greatest artists.

I thought about Picasso as my Paris friends and I traveled to the country home that they wanted my help with in Saint-Épain, a three-hour drive to the south. I thought about how I had changed my reality with art, as here I was in France, where I had not expected to be, and now I was going to change reality on a French house.

The house that my French friends had was young by the standards of Saint-Épain, at just 400 years old. It was called a troglodyte house, as it had been carved out of the limestone caves, which are soft, and so the people would turn them into homes. The one that I was in was two storeys tall, with electricity and water, and the guys had even put in a swimming pool! These little troglodyte houses dotted the countryside, built into the hillside from the caves. I had never seen anything like them, but the guys had created a charming residence offering me everything I needed to remain in the 20th century, while I played with time from long before that.

The town of Saint-Épain has been in the center of France

for 2,000 years and had seen much. It had a church, built in the 12th century CE, and which evolved as time went by, that was a marvel to me. This church was six hundred years older than the country I came from and revealed how time and its fashions had imprinted on the church, moving from Romanesque to Gothic, with the most beautiful 16th century CE oak stalls in the choir loft.

There was an oratory which had been dug in the rock of Saint-Épain in the 15th century CE, called Our Lady of Loreto. According to tradition, which I totally believed, Joan of Arc took shelter from the rain in that oratory in 1429. I was inhaling a history that was not my own, which gave me gifts everywhere I turned. I would stand staring in awe at the oratory and the locals would stop and stare at me, as if looking at me they could see the old oratory as a new miracle.

The guys wanted me to make their stone fireplace look more preserved, more connected to the house in which it existed, which meant using casein paint. Casein is an aqueous painting medium, which is made from milk, one which dates back to before we recorded history, and artists used it to paint on caves, as it is fast drying and durable.

So that's what I did. I painted their stone fireplace with casein paint. I glazed the stones of the fireplace to give them more of a sepia tone, as the stones were light in color. This allowed the stones' intrinsic light quality to show through under this semi-transparent layer of a sepia glaze. I had tweaked it in a way that looked like time had been especially gracious to it, as now those fireplace stones looked luminous, and the stained wooden mantel piece looked even darker and older. So, I changed its, and their, reality. I was painting time. As in, I was making something old look different, as if time had treated it in a way which time had most certainly not. I was altering the effects of time, just as my house painter father had done when he put a new coat of paint on a weather-beaten house.

I also changed my own reality once again, because now that I had discovered casein, I would use it in my work back at home, which would connect me back to France, and specifically, to Pablo Picasso.

Back in Utah, there's a mountainous area above Park City where the uber-wealthy reside, as the land is extraordinarily expensive, and so if you can afford the land, you can afford to put a swank house upon it. I'd snagged a job up there through a referral, and at the time, I had two jobs. One of them I was living at, because the guy who owned the house only used it during ski season, and it was not that time of year. So, I was living in the ski chalet and working at this other guy's house.

His name was Mark, and he was very interesting, as he lived in a reality in many ways all his own. He was a single guy, in his early sixties, white, and built as if he had once been a linebacker who had decided to become an accountant who was fond of jelly donuts. There was a hint of an athlete in the width of his shoulders, and the purposeful stride in his gait, but the rest of him had settled into portly late middle age.

Mark had much more money than his job seemed to allow for, as his job was to troubleshoot all of the problems the state of Utah might encounter when they were rebuilding the freeways in anticipation of the 2002 Olympics. So, in one sense, trouble was always on his mind and his job was to spot it. He was Stoic about it, and not given to outbursts, but he had a darkness which I would soon see.

He had built this old, rustic, but very expensive, log style cabin, with timbers and rock forming its very large frame. He told me that his problem was that he wanted his cabin to look older on the inside, as the newness of the sheet rock spoiled everything by revealing its age. He wanted me "to take the newness off." He wanted me to paint time.

So, I took what I had learned in France and put it to work in Park City, but in a very American fashion.

I bought an old blender at the thrift store, and then I took handfuls of ash out of the bottom of Mark's fireplace. I put the ash in my blender with a quart of buttermilk. And I blended these crazy ingredients together. It was the protein in the buttermilk that gave the paint its adhesion, just like the milk-based paint from ye olden days in France.

And so, I created this glaze and washed it over one of the cabin walls as a test. It was like magic. It looked like these walls had been there for 200 years. Mark was delighted and gave me the go ahead to do all the walls.

So, I got on with it, and then his mood began to darken. The more progress I made, the more annoyed he seemed, though he never said anything to me. He had a fellow who did all of his organizational work, and who Mark, charmingly, called "My Man Saturday," as it signaled the guy had to work on weekends.

So, I approached Man Saturday, and asked him, "What's up with Mark? I mean, it seems like I have done something to annoy him. Do you know what?"

Man Saturday seemed relieved by my question. "Okay," he said, "I can tell you that his job, which he delights in, is to scrutinize everyone and everything. And he likes to point out the flaws. He's having a tough time finding something wrong with you and your work."

I was amazed. I was doing top notch work for this guy, and he was upset because there was nothing wrong with it. The psychology of it was mind boggling, but then again, so was that of Secret Service Agent Roger who defended my artistry in court and became a friend. I also wanted to finish the job, and get paid, so I asked Man Saturday what I should do.

"If you want to have a good relationship with him, then leave him something wrong to discover on his own, and then let him just jump your ass over it. And then you apologize. And after that, you'll get along famously."

Man Saturday was telling me to make a mistake so Mark

could see this false reality as legitimate, take action, get the upper hand, and think he had created a new reality. My creation of the Russ Swain $20 was a lot simpler in its motivation, but I said sure, I would give it a shot. I was now curious.

What I did was this. I said, "Mark, let me let me tell you, I didn't get any sleep last night, you know, too much coffee, too close to bedtime. So, I feel like I'm sleepwalking. You better look around to make sure I have covered everything."

He pushed back, and said, "Everything looks fine."

I had built that reaction into my plan, and so I said, "Well, I just finished the bathroom. Would you go in and take a look?" I had glazed three walls, but I didn't touch the fourth.

Again, he said, "I'm sure it's fine," but I kept pushing, that I needed his keen eye on it, so he went into the bathroom and saw that I didn't even touch this wall.

"You said this was done?" he said, his tone now like an annoyed boss.

And then I fell on my sword. "Oh my God," I said, "I must be some kind of idiot. I can't believe that I missed the whole wall. Let me fix it and please accept my apology."

You might be surprised to learn that even such a nakedly obvious ploy like missing an entire wall would not work, but work it did, and from then on, we got along famously. And now, he opened up a bit to me.

"You have connections in the art world, right Russ?"

I said that I did.

He nodded, pleased that he was right about me. "Well, I want you to keep your eyes open, as the thing I always wanted was an original Picasso. In fact, I want one to hang right there, over the baby grand piano."

I thought about that request. He wanted a Picasso, it seemed, to complete his music room, and of course, to show people he could afford a Picasso. I just didn't know anyone who was selling one, and I wasn't connected to the criminal world in such a way that I could make a couple of phone calls and have one stolen.

So, I measured this space on the wall. I thought, "Okay, if the painting were large, it would anchor the baby grand beautifully. If he loves Picasso, then I'll do one."

I went back and found a reference work on Picasso's art and thumbed through until I saw a painting with strong primary colors, which is what the room needed.

I had an opaque projector. So, I slid my book with the Picasso painting onto the opaque projector and adjusted it to the right size for Mark's wall. I thought, well, if you want a Picasso, it has to look good and it has to have vibrant colors, as some of Picasso's work is dark and kind of drab, in fact.

I liked this painting because it was symmetrical, as the woman in the colored hat's two eyes are where eyes usually are, which was unique for Picasso. It had bright primary colors, and it really popped. I was thinking, all right, Mark, if you want a Picasso, this is as close as you're going to get to one that looks good in your room. Indeed, it looks kind of ultra-modern against a traditional setting.

I wish I had a photograph of what I did so you could see for yourselves, but take it on faith that I was not going to present a shoddy Picasso to a guy like Mark. In fact, I was very proud of what I had painted. You could say that I got blisters from patting myself on the back.

I showed up at Mark's "log cabin" with this Picasso.

I just wanted to give it to him in appreciation for the work he had provided for me.

"My God, you found one!" he exclaimed.

I replied, "Well, actually, I found a reference to one. But I copied it line for line, stroke for stroke. Exactly." I had created a perfect Picasso save for one detail: I had not signed it as Picasso. I had not signed it all.

On hearing this, Mark's fleshy face puffed into anger, and the darkness rose. "You mean that you're telling me it's worthless?" he grumbled, scowling now at a painting that moments earlier had filled him with delight.

I was offended by this remark. "It's not worthless," I said, thinking of the time and talent I had put into doing this painting. I told him that even though this was a gift, I wanted it to look like it was real. People see what they expect to see, and I didn't want anyone who came into his house to question its provenance. I had done my homework, from the kind of canvas Picasso had used, to his choice of sable brushes. I had put work into this gift.

Picasso's brush strokes were works of art, in and of themselves. So my brushstrokes had to be refined, strong, devoid of any tentativeness that can come when you are copying a great work. The brushstrokes had to flow from the focal point, which is the woman's eyes, and then out toward the edges of the canvas. I was proud of this painting, so I said to Mark, "You wanted to have a Picasso, and now you have one."

He grew even more upset. "I didn't want one because I love his work, or anything like that," he replied. "I don't know anything about his work. I do know that he's the most famous painter in the world and I wanted the prestige of owning a Picasso." Then he looked dismissively at me. "You're just a house painter and you painted this. I wanted something that nobody else could afford."

I saw that he was a deeply troubled person who was governed by an insecurity that defined his life and which I could not change.

I could get angry and stomp out, but that would not help Mark to see his new reality. So, I gently replied, "Well, the painting is not totally worthless. Because you have to consider the motivation that I had to make this gesture of friendship and appreciation."

He thought about that as he looked at the painting. Then he took it and held it up on the wall where he had planned for his "real" Picasso to hang. He turned to me and said, "Well, until I find something more suitable, you know? But it does look good there."

He never found anything more suitable.

As I thought about it, I concluded that if he wanted a Picasso so badly, then I would just go sign it. Who would know the difference? He's got the money to afford one, and his guests will think that he owns one. Nobody would have the audacity to question its authenticity, or the expertise to spot that it was a copy. I mean, I couldn't even tell, and I made the copy!

And to be shamelessly honest, part of my thinking was that if I signed the painting, then maybe I would get some more work or a referral. I did not think I was trying to send a fake Picasso into the world as a real one. I was just trying to finish my act of changing this guy's reality—or completing his illusion, as some might put it.

Picasso actually has a lovely signature. In fact, when Picasso signed a check, no one would cash it! They wanted to save his signature, which is very artistic. He wants you to know that he is responsible for what you are looking at. There is none of this squiggly line signature that goes up and down the canyon. I perfected it.

And I signed my painting as done by Pablo Picasso.

I told Mark why I had chosen to do this. "You want the prestige of owning a Picasso and now you do. You just don't have to tell anyone of its origins and just let them assume it's a genuine Picasso. And leave it at that."

He had this narrow lens at which he looked at the world and wanted the world to look back and grant him the prestige of owning something that no one else in the room, now gazing upon it, could afford. I had already changed the reality in his home by making his walls seem old. What was the difference with this painting? I wasn't trying to sell it to a gallery. I had done it out of appreciation and signed it because that was the reality he needed. And voila, Mark now had a Picasso.

I thought back to my friend Russ Swain's $20s. As long

as you perceive that the government printed them, then they are worth $20, even though it actually costs the U.S. government sixteen cents to make a $20 bill. If you think that some obscure printer made them in his little shop, it's not worth so much. Unless you can't tell the difference. Unless both seem real to you.

So, my Picasso hung on his wall, admired by many, and Mark got the prestige that he wanted. I did not stay in touch with him, but about a decade later, he sold the home. He left my name with the new owner as someone to contact should anything need to be touched up with my reality-altering skills.

The new homeowner called me to come over and do a touch up, and I was surprised to see that my Picasso was still there, as was the baby grand. Everything else had been moved out. I asked the new homeowner about the painting and the piano, and this is what he said.

"You know what, I loved the relationship between that painting and the piano, the way that piano anchors it, and, and the scale of both the way they fit this room. So, I told Mark 'I'll take the house if you leave the piano and the painting, and all the rest of the stuff you can clear out here because I have my own furniture.'"

Did Mark add the price of a "real" Picasso to the sale price of his house? I don't know, but I am pretty sure he didn't give it away, the way I had given it away to him. But I do know that guy who bought the house from him thought he was buying a real Picasso, and I did not tell him otherwise. That was now his reality, and he was happy.

I moved on. I was getting a lot of referrals from clients and designers, who liked my intricate *faux* finish work. "*Faux*" means "false" in French, so again, it's using art to change reality. Let's say a client had an ordinary white door that they wanted to make look as if made from lush maple. I would put the woodgrains and stains and the knots on the door, and the white door was no more. It was maple.

I also used a medium density fiberboard, or MDF. It's a particle board that you can marbleize. You sand it, prime it, and say you're making it white. You paint the white background color and then you pour on streaks of color to make the streaks in the marble, and then brush the streak to blend it in. Then you wax it and make it shine and it looks like it came out of 16th century Italy.

It was time to take the work a step further. I wanted to create the same kind of depth and richness that you would create in a painting. To do it, I wanted to apply the same artistic principles that I worked with when doing a painting onto someone's walls—an even bigger canvas!

The important thing is that I wanted a color palette that was balanced. I believe you can create a sense of metaphysical calm, as did the artist Mark Rothko, by layering paint to warm and cool each other to create what's called "spectral balance" because it balances the color palette across the spectrum.

It's kind of like when you're making a salad. You might put in some mandarin oranges or something sweet. Then you want to throw in some spinach leaves to give it a bit of a bitter taste to balance the soft, sweet mandarin oranges. Then you throw in some walnuts to add crunch, because you're searching for balance.

It's the same thing with art and color. Before you use greens, you have to include the opposite on the color wheel for balance, some reds and oranges. Because your eye is looking for that satisfaction of knowing that everything in that painting is composed and held together by a juxtaposition of opposites.

You could create that same kind of complexity on a wall, I learned, by doing some dark rich undertones. And then layering things out, and then putting a glaze on to create luminosity, which is basically like a filter, like sunglasses, so that light has to go through this semi-transparent layer of film, to get to the colors beneath it, which make it beautiful.

And it really shows off well, whether it's art, or a wall, or a nice piece of furniture.

So, I was working on changing the reality at another rich guy's house. He was a urologist, and he wanted me to *faux* finish his walls. And so, I did the creative finish on the walls, and I grained all of his doors and baseboards to make them look like redwood. Then he said he needed a painting to fit over his mantelpiece. I told him he wouldn't find one in a gallery that would like anything but a postage stamp, given the scale of his home, with its vast walls and high ceilings, and massive mantelpiece. "Well, what do I do?" he asked me, and of course, I knew the answer.

"We have to make one that fits the scale."

He said, "What if I just give you the green light to create something like that?"

I said, "I'd love that."

And now I had to do it, to create a reality that would fit on his wall. What would I do?

I have always loved a challenge, as you know, and so now I had one. To create not only a painting that would fit the space, but one that would make a statement.

I was inspired by a high-end furniture builder who had a shop in Park City. I was mesmerized by these little artistic renderings that were centered in his wooden panels. These panels were framed with little moldings, and they looked awesome. I knew that he had built them, but they looked like they were two hundred years old because he put a thin layer of plaster on a piece of cheesecloth, and then would roll it up and, and make the plaster crack and break to make it look old. I'd never seen anything quite like it.

But after making several attempts at creating something similar, when I rolled-up my canvas or whatever other substrate to which I applied the plaster, it wouldn't stick after it was cracked.

So, I called the owner to get some advice and he told me, "It took me weeks to figure out how to get it to adhere!

That's a trade secret I won't share with anybody! I'm not even gonna say goodbye when I hang-up the phone!" And then he hung up the phone.

Next stop, I went to the library and started reading up on Renaissance and fresco paintings by anyone from Michelangelo to the more recent artists Diego Rivera, the Mexican mural painter who became famous in the 1930's with his social realism, and who was also the husband of the artist Frida Kahlo. I learned that the simple ingredient that was missing to create adherence was just like the one I had used on the walls of Mark's house: protein. So, I started with buttermilk and bacon grease, and hoped it didn't smell when it was applied. I mixed it into the plaster, and it worked beautifully, and did not smell like breakfast. Since then, I've learned that mixing protein powder works even better. It was another kind of magical diamond dust.

There was a big old piece of fabric that wasn't canvas that was lying about. I covered it with my protein plaster, using a wetting agent, and when it dried, I just grabbed one end of it, and I tightly rolled it up to make the plaster break and crack.

So, now I had this old "canvas" to paint on, one formed of shattered plaster that made it look old.

The next thing that I needed to do was to create a painting worthy of its "age." This gig was back at a time when a Tuscan look was very popular. I had found a catalog from Christie's Auction House that featured the work of William-Adolphe Bouguereau, an artist who was born in France in 1825, and who studied in Rome in the mid-19th century. He was an academic artist, known really as a salon painter, but his work was terrific, and not widely known other than by academics and people like me.

Christie's was selling one of his paintings that had been in somebody's private collection, and the owner had died. His estate was selling the painting, so I reckoned that it had hung in some grand room of the deceased's house and would have been seen only by a few.

The picture in the brochure from Christie's has exactly the kind of happy peasant mood we were looking for. I copied that painting stroke for stroke on top of this broken plaster that looked like a fresco.

My painting looked old because of the broken plaster on which I painted, but then to age it even more, I put a nice traditional oil-based wood stain on it as a glaze. It looked as if Bouguereau had done a spell in Utah and left this behind.

The painting was big, seven feet tall and five feet wide. They trucked it over to the guy's house, and we glued it to the wall, so it would be flat and rigid. Then we had a large frame built by a picture frame house, which they screwed into the wall around the painting. It looked right at home, according to the scale of the house, which was so big you could have played roller hockey in the living room with six players aside.

And the deep rich colors of the background of the wall behind the painting that I had done kind of flowed into the painting and connected with it, so it felt right. The guy who had commissioned it absolutely loved it. "You're brilliant, Mr. Swain!" is what the good doctor pronounced. I was not going to disagree. I was very proud of this painting.

Then something extraordinary happened. This urologist loved the painting so much that his own creativity kicked in, and it certainly exceeded mine.

He was hosting guests at a party, and they all marveled at this grand painting over his fireplace. No one had ever seen anything like that, except in a triptych, or those large three-paneled pieces often found on church altars. They wanted to know about its provenance, and so he told them that it was an original work by Russ Swain from Ogden, Utah.

I jest, of course. He told them that the painting had hung in an Austrian castle for nearly a century before the Nazis stole it as they plundered art wherever they went. He spun this elaborate tale around how, at the end of the war, this painting was in a Nazi train car that was intercepted by the

Americans, who were an army unit and not an art unit, so they stashed the art along with other booty in barrels and went on their way to conquer the Nazis.

This guy said he had bought one of these barrels, and inside it was that painting. He started researching and discovered that the painting was considered a national historic treasure by Austria. The stubborn Austrians would not let that painting out of the country, yet our urologist had ownership of it. So, what was he to do?

He buried it in a big barrel of wheat is what he did, and had it shipped to the U.S.A as agriculture, and now, thanks to his own cunning and his love of art, here it was on this wall. The guests all stared at him and the painting with their eyes wide and their mouths open.

He loved telling this yarn about the painting so much that he kept embellishing and adding to it—the Nazis who stole the painting tried to fight off the Americans to protect it, and the Americans had to shoot them all. The painting was splattered with Nazi blood, which had been removed by offended Austrians, but you could still see a hint of it on the woman in the painting's skirt, which of course was very dark, and you could make anything seem like a bloodstain if you were committed to that play.

If he had written his story into a book about the origin of this painting it would have been one of the great untold tales of the rescue of a masterpiece. But he didn't, so no one could check its veracity, except the people who heard the tale.

I had been freed to create a beautiful reality, and so had the good doctor. Mine was truer than his, in that it was an accurate rendering of a real painting. What you saw is what you saw. What he said, however, was in no way true, but just like people looking at the painting believed it was real, those hearing his story believed it was real as well. Why wouldn't it be?

He eventually sold the house, and another man and his wife bought it. The husband, who was in his early fifties, and some kind of finance guy, didn't really like the style of the house but his wife did, so there they were. The one thing that he did love was my painting, and how it filled the room. He invited me over to consult on how I might change the reality of his house. He told me, "I am going to redo every room in the house except the living room, because I love that painting over there."

I don't know who told him, but he said, "I understand that you were the one who actually painted it."

I didn't know if he was also some kind of art crime cop, but I had to tell him the truth because I was proud of my work. "Yes," I said. "That's me."

He smiled and looked at the painting again, and then looked at me. "Would you just put your signature on it?" he asked. "I'm not under any illusion that it's anything other than a creative person's rendition of a piece of art. And I'd like to have you take credit for your beautiful work."

So, I signed it. "Russ Swain."

I had come, in a way, full circle, as my creation of a new reality was now publicly my own reality. I had done this painting, it had lived for a while as a fictional reality, and now it had reconnected to its origin. With me. I felt as though I had worked backstage all my life and could now come out and take a bow.

Not too long ago as I was thinking about this story I would tell you, I drove up to that house to see if the painting was still there. I clocked the "No Trespassing" sign and thought, well, if I get shot it's for a good reason—art—and then I knocked on the door. The man who I had last seen maybe twenty years ago answered the door and regarded me with a "What are you doing on my porch on a Sunday morning?" look in his eyes. I told him who I was and why I was there. I was the guy who signed his painting. He smiled in recollection, and he immediately opened up.

"When I bought this house, I loved that painting. I'd never seen anything like it. And it was huge. It looked like an

Italian fresco, the way that it was painted on plaster that was cracked and so forth."

He paused, savoring the memory of the first time he had seen the painting. "I tore down every wall in the house except for the one that that painting was on because I loved it so much." Then his voice dropped to almost a whisper. "But my lovely wife had grown tired of it and wanted to do something more with the trend of what was happening. And the trend out here is people didn't want that kind of European look that was so in vogue for so many years, they wanted something that's not so... stimulating." He looked like he was going to spit in disgust. "They want something neutral."

So, in pursuit of that tepid neutrality, the man's wife had my Bouguereau painting painted over to match the rest of the house. What had been a splendid scene of an Italian mother holding her child was now just another white wall. It had achieved a new reality by disappearing. It was literally whitewashed. And only this guy and I knew what its reality looked like before it was changed. As I drove home, I thought of that Asian proverb which says there are three deaths in a human life. There's death when you die, death when you are buried, and your final death is when your name is last repeated on the planet.

The only Russ Swain original out there was no more.

But I was still here, and I knew that there were more Russ Swain originals to come. I still had more diamond dust to sprinkle on the world.

10

All the Rest

When I say things come full circle, I guess I mean that the past realities of your life never really go away. They just pop up infused with the spirit of now, and present you with a choice: engage, or do not. It is, as it was at the beginning of this story, all about how you see things.

My mother Melba, who taught me art, and taught a couple of generations of Ogden, Utah kids art in the public schools, outlived my father by twenty-five years. I was planning a trip with my daughters to San Francisco to see *Phantom of the Opera* and went to see my mother before we left.

She had turned 90, and was happy and vital and upbeat, and we had one of our best conversations. She said to me, "It's interesting, there comes a point in your life journey, where you realize the treasure that you're looking for is discovered in the moments and the connections you have in your relationships with people."

I thought about that and asked her about something I had always wondered about. Did she miss not staying with the people she had met in California? Did she miss not working for Disney and making that connection her life treasure?

She smiled at me like I was her slightly dimwitted angel boy. "I do not, as we would not be here now. You and my granddaughters are where my treasure lives, and of course, my family."

She continued. "Your treasure lies not in seeking material goods and money and so forth," she said. "That's fool's gold. Our treasure is really all in our relationships."

I said, "Well, you've certainly been a treasure for me," and she said the same to me. It was a reassurance to each other that we had found our treasure. What we've got in our connection. And I also felt more than forgiven for my counterfeit crimes; she assured me of her love for me.

So, I went to San Francisco to see a musical, and when I came back to Ogden, my mother was gone. She had died of a heart attack while I was away. But I had that wonderful last conversation with her, that I didn't know was final when I had it, but then, you never know, do you? All I know is that before she died, my mother sprinkled her own diamond dust on me.

Of course, I wish she had lived forever, but as the saying goes, "If wishes were horses, beggars would ride." I inherited a treasure from her, that being her artistic genes, and this treasure allowed me to create a new reality for her, after she had left us. And a way for her to live forever.

I was doing this very popular kind of Tuscan *faux* finish for more wealthy people in Utah. Tuscany is a region of Italy which is famous for its architecture, and its food, and its art, and its rich history. There was a time in the early 2000s when people wanted to bring the warmth of a Tuscan villa into their Utah homes, and I was the Go-To guy.

To create a Tuscan *faux* finish, you need to first lay down a base coat. Then you overlay the base with color to create the *faux* Tuscan. I had perfected a technique that created depth and richness through deep undertones. By this I mean that you create layers of warm and cool colors to establish what's called spectral balance. I mentioned this earlier when talking about where and how I learned how to do this.

It's gorgeous. The color palette is balanced across the spectrum, but in its neutrality, it shouts vibrancy and complexity because of the depth of the colors. And so, mixing them this way made a nice Tuscan finish on Utah walls. So, while I was doing this job, the older woman in whose home I was working said to me, "My art teacher when I was growing up was Melba Swain. Was that any relation to you?"

I told her that yes, she was my mother. And that she was no longer with us, here on earth.

"I am so sorry to hear that," the woman said, and paused, her eyes closed as if in prayer. "She was a very lovely thing," she continued, her eyes now open and traveling back in time, and her face spreading with a smile. "You know, when my parents went to Back to School Night, this would have been in the 1950s, your mother took this little painting that I had done of a tree and brought it out and laid it before my parents. And she said what a magnificent job I had done, and how artistic I was, and that my parents should encourage me to pursue my artistic talents." She smiled broadly at this memory of hearing this report from her parents.

And then she grew very serious. "And your mother said, all of a sudden, and very seriously, that I wasn't just a student, I was an artist. My teacher had recognized it in me. I was in a league with artists rather than in a league of students. And she completely changed my view of myself to the point that I became an art major when I was in college. But then I realized I wouldn't have a clue how to make a living doing art, and so I gave up on it. But your lovely mother did give me a deep, deep appreciation for art. She was my favorite teacher of all the ones I ever had. And I would love to own one of her paintings."

Then the woman smiled at me as if she'd just had the

best idea ever.

"You must have access to all of her paintings, as her son. There must be so many."

I wracked my brain to think if there were any of my mother's paintings left behind. She had given some as gifts to friends and relatives, but there were none of them stashed in a vault, waiting to be sprung. My mother devoted so much time to her students that she didn't have time to paint that much, other than to do demonstrations in her class. But I knew, as well as I knew my own name, what I had to do next.

I smiled expansively back at her. "Well, you're in luck, ma'am. I do have access to the archive of my mother's paintings. And I am delighted to hear that you would like one. Where would you like this painting to hang?"

I was suddenly back in the zone of the huge Bouguereau painting I had created to fill the enormous space over that guy's mantelpiece in Park City. If I saw the space, I would see the painting.

The woman showed me where she wanted the painting to hang. I measured it and thought the size of the painting that I needed to fit would be 37 inches by 28 inches.

"I think I have a couple of paintings that will fit perfectly," I said. "What subject matter are you thinking of?"

The woman looked delighted. "Did she ever paint Indians?" She meant Native Americans, but she was of that generation that used a term that we had abandoned, unless we were speaking about people who actually lived in India. But I plugged into her vernacular and replied, "Oh, yes, of course, she painted Indians all the time."

I was looking around at the colors on her wall to see what I wanted to float through the painting, the tans and reds and dark greens. I thought, yeah, okay, well, this is easy.

So, I went home and trawled through my reference books, and found a painting of a noble Native American sitting on his horse, looking at the mountains in the distance. It was by an artist who had been dead for more than a century, so I was safe. And I set to work.

I used the basic structure of the painting to lay it out, and then using oil paint, made those mountains look like the majestic Wasatch, which we gazed upon in Ogden. I turned the dial to add some of my mother's spirit to warm it all up, even though it was a scene set in summer. And then I signed it with my mother's signature, one I knew so well from forging notes from her to the principal back in high school. So now we had a Melba Swain painting out there in the world. We had a new reality.

I took the painting to the woman who wanted it and told her I had found it in my mother's archives. Would it suit her purposes?

"Oh my gosh, it's perfect," she exclaimed in delight. "It's like it was meant to be!"

And that's how it felt to me. My mother, who had nurtured this woman's love of art, was connecting with her once again, through me. God works in mysterious ways, as they say, but I would have been even more grateful if God sent some cash my way. My mother had always said a "picture is worth $1000" so that's what I asked for this painting, and that's what I got.

Soon, I was in the Melba Swain painting business. A friend of the woman who bought the "Indian" painting, who was also an elderly former student of my mother, contacted me. She asked me, "Did your mother ever do paintings of the Weber River?"

The Weber is a 125-mile-long river that begins its flow in the northwest of the Uinta Mountains and empties into the Great Salt Lake. It passes to the west of Ogden and is one of the most beautiful spots in the world.

"Yes, she did," I replied. "She painted it in all the seasons. Which one are you thinking of?"

"Oh my gosh," she said, "I would love to have a painting of the Weber River in winter."

I smiled and nodded. "How I remember my mother

trudging through the winter snow carrying her easel and her paints. She followed her artistic soul to find the right place to capture the Weber River no matter how cold it was." I paused, seeing the dramatic scene in my mind's eye. Then I returned to practical matters. "Where do you plan to hang this painting?"

"Oh, I think it would look nice above my couch."

In the art world, we call that hanging an "OTC", which means "over the couch", and the dimensions are easy. No bigger than your average couch.

"Let me go rummage through her archives," I said. "It will take me about a week as they are extensive, and her filing system was, well, shall we say, that of an artist, and not an accountant."

"That's just great," she said, delighted.

I had one more question for her. "What color are your walls?"

"Green."

I smiled. White snow, green trees, Weber River. Piece of cake. And another $1,000.

If anybody wanted one of my mother's paintings, I produced them. I thought if it makes these elderly ladies happy and gives them a connection to a teacher they loved, and makes them feel like they've got an heirloom, that would be good. And to me, it honored my mother's devotion to art, and gave her life a new reality. It also kept me afloat, financially, which my mother would have wanted. She knew that we may be each other's treasures, but we also needed some of the earthly ones to get by, as we made our way.

Fortunately, none of "my mother's" customers ever wanted to make a trek to check out the archives. Otherwise, I would have to start a fire (or news of one) that tragically turned all my mother's art into ash.

Which, given that the sun which gives us life is one day going to burn out, all art will eventually become. Or as the Book of Ecclesiastes puts it: time and chance happeneth to them all."

It's a beautiful perspective on pretty much everything, and while it is the ending for everyone, time and chance still has the capacity to surprise. It certainly did for me when a knock came to my door. I opened it to see my old high school principal, Cluff (yes, his name) Snow, standing on the front porch. "Principal Snow!" I said. To what do I owe this surprise visit? Am I in some kind of trouble again?"

I had spent a lot of time in his office when I was busted in high school for forging report cards and absence excuse notes from parents. At the time, Principal Snow was pretty biblical in his opinion of where I would wind up if I continued down this path. And now he had wound up at my door.

"Rusty Swain," he mused, using the name of my youth, and staring at me as though he had once memorized every feature of my face. He was grayer, and heavier, but still had that athletic swagger of the star quarterback he had been in college.

With a sardonic smile at me, Principal Snow declared, "You're still in the same trouble you were in, back in those days at Ogden High School! Do you see these few white hairs, still remaining on my head? You put 'em there, with all that mischief you got into! But I have brought you some good news, Rusty. I'm bringing you a chance to atone."

A chance to atone. He was back to the Bible. I was hooked. I mean, who wouldn't want that kind of chance, especially if you were me, but how was my high school principal going to deliver it?

Back in the early forties, Principal Snow had quarter-backed his college team to win the state championship. After graduating, he became the football coach of the newly constructed Ogden High School. He instituted a yearly competition between Ogden High and Weber High and he designed a trophy made of an earthen jug with a cork stopper. He hired an artist to paint it with a plaque on it that read, "The Little Brown Jug, Champions."

The trophy jug was passed between the schools which competed for it, for a couple of decades. One year, however, fights broke out between the rival schools and the competition was canceled. At some point in the 1960s, Coach Snow became Principal Snow, until he retired at some point, in the 1980s.

In his retirement, he wondered what had happened to the jug trophy, since it was a part of Ogden High School's history, and it deserved a place of honor in the trophy case. It became his personal quest, as he sought to find it.

He queried retired teachers and janitors for months until he got a tip that it might be in the basement storage room of the county library. He rummaged through dozens of boxes until finally, he found it. But shortly after word got out that he had found it, Weber High School made a claim for it, citing that they had won more games than Ogden had, and so the trophy should be in their trophy case.

Principal Snow would be damned if he'd let them have his beloved trophy. So, he hatched a plan to take revenge. He needed a counterfeiter or forger who could make an exact replica of the trophy, exhibiting the wear and stains that had occurred over decades of changing hands. He remembered a good one. He remembered me.

So here he was in my living room, sharing an iced tea with his former miscreant student, imploring me to summon my dark arts to make an exact forgery of the Little Brown Jug which he would, in turn, present to those godless sonsabitches at Weber High who wanted to steal his masterpiece of a trophy, and return the original to Ogden High. That was it. Produce a duplicate trophy to allow for the switch and all would be forgiven. I would be redeemed.

How could I refuse such an offer? The clink of our glassware sealed our agreement.

I got to work, and it was not a tough job. I found a brown jug in a hardware store, with a cork stopper, the very same size that Principal Snow had bought decades ago. I aged it with my various glazing techniques and used the same skills at hand-lettering that had once fooled the principal to create the plaque. A month after we had clinked our iced tea glasses, a beaming Principal Snow presented a lovely, old-looking, jug trophy to his rival principal at Weber High School, who accepted it with a smugness that he will surely regret when he reads these words.

The real trophy sits today in a specially made trophy case, inside the teacher's lounge at Ogden High, with a plaque, dedicating it to Principal Snow for his years of dedication and service.

I had again created a new reality for people to believe, and they did, until now. So, you can consider this both an atonement, and an approved confession, as I promised Principal Snow that I would not say a word so long as he walked the earth. He left us about a decade ago, so the word has now been said.

One of the great things about the computerization of art is that it drove me away from graphic design and back to my first love: painting. And I actually got to connect with a real art gallery because of my *faux* finishing, in a way that created a crazy new reality for art because of my art, along with a very cool powder room. Let me explain.

I was working for a man named Don Simpson and his wife, Olivia. They owned an art gallery in Santa Fe, New Mexico, and lived in Park City. I did their Utah walls, giving them a cool wash of grays, and then a wash of yellow ochres. It looked deep and rich and multi-layered, and the effect created luminosity, which is the way that light passes through a semi-transparent layer of film to get to the colors beneath.

You put a beautiful French armoire in front of a wall that I have finished like that, and it makes the armoire the star of the show. It shows it off as if it were the focal point of a painting. So, it's like the walls become a backdrop of a canvas painting that shows off the objects that you want to draw your attention to.

Don Simpson and his wife were delighted. Indeed, Don had an epiphany. When he saw his art on the walls that I had finished in his house he said, "All of my art looks like it belongs here. You need to come to Santa Fe."

Don and Olivia's gallery in Santa Fe was struggling. The art was not selling. So, Don wanted me to do for his New Mexico art gallery what I had done for his Utah house. So, I flew down to Santa Fe for a weekend, and painted one of his gallery walls. About a month later, he called me and said, "Russ, you have to come back to Santa Fe and paint all the walls in my gallery. The wall that you have done just brings everything into a rich look of harmony. The paintings on it look wonderful, but they fall flat on the white wall. So please come in and paint all of my walls like the one you have already done as soon as you can. Because right now, the only paintings that are selling are on the wall you painted."

It was a stunning admission. I had altered the reality of a wall in an art gallery to make the art hanging upon it be seen in a new way. I had created a new reality for art, and people now wanted to pay for it.

The gallery in Santa Fe was similar to Para Graphics in that it, too, was in a strip mall, but that was because rent in Santa Fe was really expensive. Unlike my strip mall, there were high end little shops flanking it, like the high-end tobacco shop that sold expensive cigars. So, there were people around who bought expensive things, and could come and shop.

The gallery sold old paintings. It sold all kinds: some artists might do landscapes and others, portraits, while some did abstract. So, my challenge was to get the walls to enhance any kind of art. I needed diamond dust.

I knew that wood tones are something that everybody has in their home. Everything is about relationships, and you want to create a relationship with the objects, whether it's to your wood cabinets, or the or even your wooden picture frame. So, taking that relationship note as my cue, I thought I would start with a deep rich, kind of a mahogany wood tone, a bass note, to create shadow.

Then I took a yellow ochre and washed it over the entire wall in a semi transparent layer, so that those shadows that I just put down showed up from behind it. Next, I created harmony by scuffing a transparent layer of grayish taupe over what was already there, but still allowed the colors below to break through very abstractly, and subtly.

I added a semi-transparent base of white to wash them all, so now you had this layering of colors that just seemed to dance atop one another. And, and then when that dried, I took just a little bit of raw umber, in a clear base, and washed the whole thing. It was like putting on a pair of dark glasses to look at it because it creates that thing that we artists love so much: luminosity.

It creates depth and richness and light and it's just magical. If you hang a painting on that kind of wall, you're going to see the colors of that wall floating through the painting and back out onto the wall. And that's what Don and Olivia absolutely loved.

Olivia then had a very different task for me, back in Utah. She wanted me to change the reality of her powder room. She said, "We entertain a lot. I want to make that powder room look as inviting as can be, so it takes off the stress of having to use someone's bathroom."

And I said, "So, let's do some art on the walls with some with some quotes. You know, like, for example, if you love Albert Einstein, we will do some quotes about Einstein and a rendering of Einstein and so on."

She loved that idea. So, I ended up doing some calligraphy on the powder room wall of quotes that she liked. And I said, "If somebody has to use your restroom, and they're doing something that's taken a long time, they can come out and say, 'I was just so charmed by all of the art and brilliant quotes on the wall and, and so forth."

She reported back to me a couple of months later, and said, "Out of everything that you've done in my home, that guest powder room is the crowd pleaser. That's what knocks out all of my guests. The thing I love is that it's so nice to have that thing that hits people as a surprise." Then she paused and said, "And I will tell you a secret. Every morning I get up and I take my Cosmopolitan magazine in there, and that's my meditation room. My kids, everybody knows that's mom's time to be alone. Don't bug her, she's in the bathroom. She's going to be there for a good 25 minutes. And we don't disturb Mom as she gathers her thoughts and gets ready for the day. And then she comes out and she's in a good mood." She told me that my powder room had become the heart of her house. Diamond dust.

I also got the chance to try my hand once again at penmanship. I worked for a doctor from Armenia and painted his clinic with really complicated faux finish work. I had a couple of employees helping me, so I told the doctor that I had to be paid on Friday, because I had to make payroll.

He agreed but said that I had to be at his office at exactly 12 o'clock on Friday, as he was leaving town for two weeks. So I met him at the time he commanded, and he handed me a check. And he said, "Good luck."

I took the check to the bank and the bank would not cash it because there was no signature. That's what his "good luck" had meant. My employees asked me what I was going to do. I said, "Well, it's just a signature. All we have to do is find a copy of his signature."

So, we went back to his clinic and jumped in the dumpster behind it. I and my two employees were going through everything in that cursed dumpster. And one of the guys said, "Bingo, I found a prescription thing that he had to discard that he had signed."

I grabbed it, and forged his signature on the check, I took

it to the bank, and they cashed it. My employees asked if I was afraid that he was going to come back at me for forging his signature. I had no fear, because for him to do so would be an admission of his guilt.

The next time I saw him, he just looked at me with a wry smile and said, "I think you're finally starting to understand me." I actually did more work for him because he liked my work, and because he was embarrassed. But once again, my past exploits in forgery paid off.

Today, I mostly paint murals in people's homes, some of them designed to be what they are, like a sunset on a wall, or some of them designed to fool the eye, in the trompe l'oeil style I mentioned earlier. I painted from references in books and online, but the aim was always the same: to create a trompe l'oeil not so much to fool your eye, but to create a "wow" factor.

I painted a collection of wine bottles in a mural in a client's bar, with the client's name on them, to suggest his vineyard had produced these bottles which, of course, you could not sip from. And to make his bar look like the showcase for this amazing vineyard.

One client had trouble getting her young son to close the bathroom door after he used it, so I painted a tree growing from the wall and over the bathroom door, to remind the boy to close the door—and so put the tree back together.

Another client had a round recessed ceiling with a small chandelier hanging from it. It was too small for the scale of the house, so I painted a simple ship's compass up in the recessed ceiling, and that not only solved the space problem, but it also looks really good. You look up and navigate.

One of my clients used to live in Scotland and wanted an old Scottish cottage painted on his winding staircase. Then he wanted more. He wanted Scottish ancestors in the painting, so I added a graveyard below the cottage. They didn't have to be living.

There was another client whose wife was about to celebrate her birthday, and he wanted to surprise her. She had this huge closet where she kept her massive collection of shoes and handbags, and she called the room her "kitten cave."

Her husband said, "Let's do something with the kitten cave."

Then he came up with a brilliant idea. His wife had leopard skin carpet on the floor of her kitten cave that extended to the enormous closet. "Why don't we paint a leopard stepping through the wall?" he said. "Like he's getting ready to step onto that carpet?"

I loved the idea, and so, I set to work. I could not set up shop in her kitten cave and expect the result to be a surprise, so I came up with a plan and ran it by her husband. "I'll do the painting on a canvas. And then we'll glue it to the wall and then spackle the edges of the canvas. So, it blends into the wall and then paint over it." He agreed.

I wanted to create a leopard that looked like he was stepping over the baseboard, so once I had the painting done, I had to get back into the kitten cave to set the stage, as it were, for the leopard's entry. I had to paint part of the cat's paw on the baseboard of the closet to make it look "real." I used filler to augment the baseboard, and then painted part of the cat's paw on that raised baseboard, to look as if it was really coming into the room.

So, the kitten caver's husband took her out for a long birthday lunch, and I did my work. I glued the painting of the leopard onto the closet, and I had surrounded the cat with jungle foliage, and it looked as if a leopard was really coming out of the wall.

The kitten cave owner was absolutely delighted, and once again, a reality had been changed through art.

My favorite job was this very interesting trompe l'oeil

job, one that involved painting a mural on the wall of a swimming pool. It was one of those murals that shows the ocean on one level and then what's beneath the ocean, and what's above the ocean. I had sky and islands and fish and sunken treasure painted on the pool wall to make it seem that you were swimming in the big blue sea.

The client came down and had a six-year-old granddaughter with him. He said, "Hey, I'm watching my kid today, but I need to run to the liquor store. Could you keep an eye on my granddaughter?"

I said sure, and I went back to painting. This little girl was watching me paint, and looking so curiously at what I was doing, that I said to her, "You want to paint, don't you?"

She grinned with excitement. Yes, she wanted to paint.

I thought that she could paint whatever she wanted, and I could always paint over it.

So, I made her a little palette and gave her a brush. "Don't get any paint on your clothes," I said, and let her loose. Well, she started painting, and I immediately saw that she was painting from her heart.

She painted a clownfish with polka dots and stripes on it and big eyelashes and a huge slippery tail with sparkles coming off it. I just watched her with such admiration because she was pulling something right out of the emotion of her soul and painting it on the wall and having a great time. It took me back in time to when I was that kid, making my art for the pure pleasure of it.

When the guy came back home and saw what we were doing, he was annoyed. He wanted to know why I was allowing his six-year-old granddaughter to paint on his expensive mural.

I said, "With all due respect, sir, this is the only art on this whole painting because mine is just copying some references and doing goofy stuff. But this is art. I could paint over it, but I wouldn't touch it. Let's leave it and honor your granddaughter's creative expression."

He looked at me and looked at the hopeful expression on his granddaughter's little face, and finally, he conceded. And then he did more.

For years afterward, whenever he hosted a party, he would bring guests to the pool room to show them "What my granddaughter did when she was six!." He was proud of the reality she had created on my reality. And it gave him a new way to see her reality, and so onward he went, changed by art. It's all about how you see what you're looking at. She had given her grandfather her own diamond dust.

Today, I am looking at our world through my one good eye. I have glaucoma in my right eye, and so everything looks like dappled fog through starboard. It makes judging hues very difficult. Unless, of course, I close my right eye and just look at the world through my left. Which is what I do.

You might think for an artist that this eye affliction would be terminal, but it all connects to how I began. My glaucoma has made me change the way I look at the world. Is it any less real? No, of course not. I just see it from a different perspective, and that's what seeing is all about. I believe that what I am seeing is true, and have done so all my life, because if I can touch it, I can believe it.

You have learned about all the alternative realities that I have created that became true, until some were changed again, by a school principal, by the Secret Service, by the Church of Latter-day Saints, by a guy who wanted me to sign that painting that had been rescued from the Nazis and reclaim a reality I had created. Or had we created a new one?

All I know is that my life has been sprinkled with diamond dust, and that dust has made my art luminous in a way that I could never have imagined. So, by telling you this story, I have decided that I will paint some more. I will paint some Russ Swain originals and offer them to the world as my own work. Of course, it's all my own work, but what I mean is that it will be the very thing it was meant to be, and not some other reality.

I hope that you will come with me on that journey, and that together, we can spread some more diamond dust around our world. And make it shine, even a little bit, for just a little while, so that perhaps someone can see their way out of the darkness and into the light.

EPILOGUE

Thank you, dear reader, for agreeing to come on this journey with me. Now that we have reached our destination, I wanted to let you know how we got here in the first place, with you, reading a book, about me.

This book came about due to a most unlikely friend. He said, "Look, I know that whole, weird episode in your life, has made you feel... full of doubts and self-incrimination. But write it down and put it out there. Own it. You'll discover that it has great connecting power to others."

As you have discovered, the actions I took to save my family wound up destroying my marriage. The pain of my divorce had been tempered by its inevitability, and maybe my reality is that I was never cut out to be a good husband. I am not seeking to escape blame for my actions that ended my marriage, nor attempting to revise what I have told you. I am just a better scholar of myself these days.

In the years after our divorce, my former wife and I were able to remain amicable. We got together with our daughters for Thanksgiving and Christmas, and for occasional family celebrations.

Even so, l was caught off guard during a chance encounter with her when she told me that she had met someone. "His name is Mike. I intend to marry him." She studied me for a reaction.

"I hope you'll be very happy together," I told her. "And I wish you both... the best of luck."

I was being sincere. I did want her to be happy. It just felt very sad to be saying goodbye.

"I will bid you farewell, then," I said, trying to sound nonchalant. And I turned to walk away.

"Now hold-on a second, mister! Don't you just march off! You're still the father of our kids. And you're still my friend. I know that when you meet Mike, you will like him. So don't give me this... this big old "farewell" scenario! Nobody's going anywhere. And don't curl your lip! It spoils your good looks."

With that, she gave me a friendly hug. "We'll stay in touch," she said. She then climbed into her car and drove away.

In the weeks that followed, I just kept my head in my work and tried not to think about my ex-wife's impending marriage. In fact, I learned of her wedding date, and of their honeymoon travels, from my daughters.

I was careful not to ask questions, nor intrude. Then, one day I received a call from my former wife, inviting me to come to her new home in East Bountiful, to meet her new husband. I said yes.

Immediately, I could see why she was so taken with him. He was funny and he was kind. He had charisma. Right off the bat, I liked this guy.

We relaxed into a lengthy conversation that lasted a couple of hours.

We didn't realize it at the time, but this would be a milestone moment for both of us.

In the months that followed, Mike and I became the closest of friends on many levels—as comrades, as confidants, as collaborators. On one occasion, Mike said that since we had married the same woman, at different stages of our lives, that this made us "'husbands-in-law", a term that has stayed with us ever since.

One weekend, early last spring, Mike invited me to stop by his place and join him for dinner. His wife had flown off earlier to spend a few days with her aging parents.

Over a well-cooked meal, he looked at me, his eyes flashing with an idea, and then he told me what that idea was.

"We should write a book!"

"A book? What kind of book?"

"Your story, about a guy who was driven to act—even though his actions were muddle-headed, futile and wrong. Yes, he counterfeited money! Then we'll add in those off-the-wall stories you tell me over breakfast on the weekends! It can have a serious, semi-tragic tone—I mean, it did screw-up your life. But it can also project a luster of contagious hopefulness! I've already come up with a name for the title. We'll call it Diamond Dust!"

I had only the dimmest notion that something significant might be happening.

But indeed, it was.

"What on earth do we know about writing a book?" I asked him.

"We don't know squat. But I have a friend in New York. He's a writer and he knows how to get ink onto the page."

The only hurdle we now had would be in getting my former wife and now Mike's wife to sign-off on the idea.

Someone had to let the secret out of the bottle. Mike volunteered.

One day, after breakfast, with me standing upright behind him, Mike, in a voice as soft as baby shampoo, announced our plan.

His wife regarded us with a look of compassionate dismay that she would normally reserve for only the spectacularly incompetent. After a few moments of stone silence, she spoke, her voice taking on a tin edge.

"Fine," she said. "You two go and write your silly book. But I promise you, if you mention me by name, or the names of either of our children, I will sue both of you, and hang you out to dry!"

So the lovely woman who made me a father and made Mike and I husbands-in-law has and will forever remain a mystery, dear reader. To our other friends who were not mentioned in our book, you can thank her for that.

And I thank you for taking this trip with me. As I said at the beginning of our journey, most of it is true. And all of it is real.

Russ and Mike, the husbands-in-law, seeing what they see… .